OUTER STARS

Previous Winners of the Katherine Anne Porter Prize
in Short Fiction
Polly Buckingham, series editor
Barbara Rodman, founding editor

The Stuntman's Daughter by Alice Blanchard
Rick DeMarinis, Judge

Here Comes the Roar by Dave Shaw
Marly Swick, Judge

Let's Do by Rebecca Meacham
Jonis Agee, Judge

What Are You Afraid Of? by Michael Hyde
Sharon Oard Warner, Judge

Body Language by Kelly Magee
Dan Chaon, Judge

Wonderful Girl by Aimee La Brie
Bill Roorbach, Judge

Last Known Position by James Mathews
Tom Franklin, Judge

Irish Girl by Tim Johnston
Janet Peery, Judge

A Bright Soothing Noise by Peter Brown
Josip Novakovich, Judge

Out of Time by Geoff Schmidt
Ben Marcus, Judge

Venus in the Afternoon by Tehila Lieberman
Miroslav Penkov, Judge

In These Times the Home Is a Tired Place by Jessica Hollander
Katherine Dunn, Judge

The Year of Perfect Happiness by Becky Adnot-Haynes
Matt Bell, Judge

Last Words of the Holy Ghost by Matt Cashion
Lee K. Abbott, Judge

The Expense of a View by Polly Buckingham
Chris Offutt, Final Judge

ActivAmerica by Meagan Cass
Claire Vaye Watkins, Final Judge

Quantum Convention by Eric Schlich
Dolan Morgan, Final Judge

Orders of Protection by Jenn Hollmeyer
Colin Winnette, Final Judge

Some People Let You Down by Mike Alberti
Zach VandeZande, Final Judge

They Kept Running by Michelle Ross
Polly Buckingham, Final Judge

There Is Only Us by Zoe Ballering
Polly Buckingham, Final Judge

What Did You Do Today? by Anthony Varallo
Molly Giles, Final Judge

Where to Carry the Sound by Nina Sudhakar
Molly Giles, Final Judge

The Year of Perfect Happiness by Becky Adnot-Haynes
Matt Bell, Judge

Last Words of the Holy Ghost by Matt Cashion
Lee K. Abbott, Judge

The Expense of a View by Polly Buckingham
Chris Offutt, Final Judge

ActivAmerica by Meagan Cass
Claire Vaye Watkins, Final Judge

Quantum Convention by Eric Schlich
Dolan Morgan, Final Judge

Orders of Protection by Jenn Hollmeyer
Colin Winnette, Final Judge

Some People Let You Down by Mike Alberti
Zach VandeZande, Final Judge

They Kept Running by Michelle Ross
Polly Buckingham, Final Judge

Them Is Only Us by Zoe Ballering
Polly Buckingham, Final Judge

What Did You Do Today? by Anthony Varallo
Molly Giles, Final Judge

When to Carry the Sound by Nina Sudhakar
Molly Giles, Final Judge

OUTER STARS

Stories by

KIRSTEN SUNDBERG LUNSTRUM

2025 Winner, Katherine Anne Porter Prize in Short Fiction

University of North Texas Press
Denton, Texas

Printed in the United States of America.

10 9 8 7 6 5 4 3 2 1

Permissions:
University of North Texas Press
1155 Union Circle #311336
Denton, TX 76203-5017

The paper used in this book meets the minimum requirements of the American National Standard for Permanence of Paper for Printed Library Materials, z39.48.1984. Binding materials have been chosen for durability.

Library of Congress Cataloging-in-Publication Data is available from the Library of Congress

ISBN 978-1-57441-980-1 (paper)
ISBN 978-1-57441-988-7 (ebook)

Outer Stars is Number 24 in the Katherine Anne Porter Prize in Short Fiction series

Cover image: Adam Fung. *blue moon, uncertain sky*. 2021. Oil on linen over panel, 24 x 36 in.
www.adamfung.com @adamfung.art

The electronic edition of this book was made possible by the support of the Vick Family Foundation.

For N, who is my North Star.

CONTENTS

Clean Breaks

Sonja wakes to a stranger's voice in the boat with her. A man's voice. A panicked moment passes before she realizes it's coming over the radio and not from inside the cabin.

"Aidez-moi," the man says. "Help. Ayúdame. Please." His call cuts in and out between the fuzz of the handheld VHF's granular static.

It is 2:00 a.m. on a Tuesday morning in early July. Sonja's boat is anchored in a small bay off the eastern shoreline of the Haida Gwaii archipelago of British Columbia. She goes to the porthole and spots a single yawl, small, the sails down but the cabin brightly lit and blazing streaks of white across the black-glass bay. She sees a shadow inside—a dark head and shoulders. A man.

Sonja is alone, just as she's been alone for the last week in this bay, and before that for a week in the bay just farther south, and before that in other bays along the coast that she's been slowly following north to a point she hasn't yet determined: her turnaround spot or new home, maybe Alaska—Ketchikan or Prince of Wales Island—someplace even more remote than here. She doesn't know. She's been alone for nearly fifty days, the only exceptions being two brief conversations she had at fuel docks in British Columbia on Moresby Island and at Skidegate, both with men who looked at her hard in a way she's come to expect as a woman traveling unaccompanied. Men like them can sniff out a woman's vulnerabilities. She laid cash on their counters, said as little as possible, and left—no pleasantries for them to remember later, no name; her money mixed into their tills, indistinguishable from the other bills; her boat motoring away from their docks before they could imagine a more interesting way to end the exchange.

"Please, help," the male voice repeats over her radio now, and she knows it's coming from the little yawl.

She fumbles to unfurl herself from the low-ceilinged berth, slides her feet into her rubber boots, pulls a raincoat over her nightdress.

She might just ignore it, she thinks as she prepares to leave the warmth of her boat for who-knows-what catastrophe outside. How is the man across the bay to know she's receiving his calls? It was an accident that she left her radio on overnight. These bays along the coast are silent, isolated, tucked away in deep glacial cuts between densely treed islands. There's no reason to expect company of the human sort, so she generally keeps the VHF off. She put it on the night before while she ate, though, scanning for sound to combat the unease that now and then overtakes her. She dislikes it in herself—this occasional need for the illusion of companionship—but sometimes the stillness turns animal on her, furred and thick and hungry. She can't predict its arrival, that single canine shadow that splits and splits again behind the screen of evergreens at the edge of whatever bay she's moored in until she feels encircled, trapped. It only happens in the late evening, when the darkness velvets the water and the last dim light in the sky sinks into black. She doesn't mind solitude, but this is something different—spectral and chilling. Not just loneliness, but obliteration. She can't bear it, so she turns on the VHF and searches for FM stations that reach this far. She might get classical or jazz. A public news station from Vancouver Island or southeast Alaska. Once, a tribal station was broadcasting a storytelling presentation in a language she couldn't understand. Only these human noises can send the slinking wolves retreating into the woods. Last night it wasn't a voice but Brahms. Just as good. She listened while she ate a can of beef-and-potato stew, drank a small mug of hot cider sluiced with a thumb of bourbon, and went to bed without washing up. She'd left the radio on low, only semiconscious of its company, enough to let her sleep. Now she regrets it.

"I see you. Please," the voice says.

Her heart trips. This time she picks up. "What's your location? Over." She has to be sure it's him—the man across the bay.

Static.

"Hello, copy?" she says into the radio.

"Help. Please." The voice hardens. "You're right there. Help me, please. I have a sick child on board. I have no more medicine, no fuel. Please."

Sonja lets out a long breath and drops the radio into her coat pocket. She lifts down the shotgun she keeps over the cabin door and slings it over her shoulder.

Outside the deck is damp and the air wet and chilled. The black of the water meets the black of the shore in an inky spill. These bays can be shallow bottomed or crater-like, their centers great, shapeless pits. This one is a pit. Overhead the stars seem farther away than usual, though there are more of them—so many more than she ever saw inland, where the cities exhale light in vaporous clouds that never fully dissipate. She is intensely aware of her isolation.

She untethers the dinghy from the stern, climbs down the swim ladder, and steps in. The water slaps against its aluminum side. She's learned to sit in the dinghy with her knees splayed and feet wide apart for balance as she rows. Each time she raises the oars, water beads skitter from the blades along the handles and into her coat's cuffs, trickling cold up her arms. It takes five minutes, but feels longer, for her to cross the distance between her boat and the stranger's.

As she pulls herself nearer, the man disappears from the inside and reappears on deck. He waves his arms at her, as if she has any doubt it's him in need of her help.

Thirty feet away she stops, stands up, and swivels the shotgun so it hangs over her chest. "I'll shoot if I have to," she says.

The man drops his hands. "No," he says. He has a heavy accent that she can't place. "No, please." His voice shifts. "It's my daughter."

Sonja feels a burning in her back like a wire plucked and popped. It sends fire down both arms and into the pit of her stomach. She lets go of the shotgun. "Coming aboard," she says and sits again, picking up her oars.

Sonja believes that people only choose the sort of life she's chosen if there are no other options. This has been confirmed in her year and a half of living on the water. There was the man she met in Seattle after she first bought the boat and was paying monthly for a liveaboard slip in the marina at Shilshole. He'd lost his wife to pancreatic cancer and his house to the bills for her useless treatment. He kept a blue heeler for company and spoke to the dog in a bitter, caustic tone. At the same marina she met another man—Tom—three slips from hers, who was five months sober and kind, his face soft with what she read as shame and sorrow and tentative hope. He was afraid, he told her one evening over takeout boxes of fried chicken and tall brown bottles of vanilla soda that he drank to keep from really drinking.

"Afraid of what?" she asked.

"Afraid if I live anywhere but alone on this boat, I'll kill myself."

He'd been an investment banker with an apartment downtown, a girlfriend he'd thought he would eventually marry, and a Lexus he'd totaled driving the wrong way up a freeway on-ramp at seven thirty on a Sunday morning. That was the end for him.

"Why?" she asked, and he answered in metaphors: The dogs never stopped nipping at his heels, the big hunger kept swallowing him, the black hole never bottomed out. Did she understand? She did. He had to leave it all and start over if he wanted to stay clean.

"Clean break," he said. "That's what it means." He couldn't keep pretending he wasn't terrified. He had a handsome half smile and was a good lover, patient and soft-spoken in bed, always apologetic afterward, though she assured him there was nothing to be sorry about. He liked to sleep with his hand on her bare hip, and now and then his fingers tensed as if her body were a ledge he was gripping. Eventually his need was too much. She had no interest in being claimed. Sonja left Seattle and went north.

In La Conner she met a woman who'd been jilted a week before her wedding and had left everything to move onto a thirty-foot tug. In Bellingham she met a man who'd been homeless until his brother had died and left him a thirty-six-foot sailboat. "Bastard wouldn't give me a goddamn thing when he was alive," he laughed. Sonja slept with him too, just once.

"I'm lonely," she said when she kissed him. "That's all this is." He understood and expected nothing more from her. Men who had never owned much were perhaps better at letting go.

Farther north, in Vancouver, she moored next to an old man and his teenage granddaughter. He was raising the girl to be free, he told Sonja. "Fuck the government," he said and cackled, relishing his rebellion. His boat kept him untethered, mobile, owing no one. Sonja ate tacos with him and the granddaughter one evening, then played a round of gin. The girl barely spoke. She had acne that flamed swollen and red across her cheekbones, eyes the color of a gray March sky.

Where were her parents? Sonja wondered. *Why had they let her go with this grandfather?* The girl troubled Sonja, appearing in a dream that night as a stray dog skulking around the marina. Somehow in her dream Sonja knew the dog was the girl and that she was hungry, but she didn't set out food or water. When she woke the dream's disquiet lingered through the day. *It's none of my business*, Sonja told herself, but when she and the girl ended up in the marina laundry at the same time one afternoon, the girl with her sweatshirt hood up and her earbuds in, Sonja slipped her a piece of paper that read, "If you need out, I'm in slip A24." The man's boat was gone in the morning, and the girl with it. *None of my business*, Sonja reminded herself, though for weeks she worried that she'd made things worse, or that she should have done more.

Later, when her own boat's motor broke down in Campbell River and she had to stay a month at a motel in town, she met Melora, who cleaned rooms four days a week and studied to be a sonographer the other three. They got margaritas together at a Mexican restaurant a few times, and Melora told Sonja about her ex and how he'd taken even her wedding ring when he'd left her and how what she loved most about sonography was the darkness and the silence of being with a stranger whose insides you could see. Since the ex had left her, she'd lived alone and would forever.

"How can you say forever?" Sonja asked.

"I know it in my heart, and I spend all day looking at people's hearts, so I should know." She laughed. She had the kind of laugh that seemed to break open suddenly, a cascading peal of real joy. Her short burgundy hair was damp against her temples from the heat of drinking, and her face and laugh reminded Sonja of her own grandmother's somehow, though the two women were nothing alike. She hadn't felt true comfort with another person in ages.

Melora was the only person Sonja told about Angie.

"Isn't that the saddest thing I've ever heard," Melora said after the whole story was out. She slid her hand across the sticky table and laid it on top of Sonja's. "God, honey. That's just the saddest thing I've ever heard."

The next day Sonja's boat was ready, and she didn't hang around to say good-bye.

Now, in the dark, her heart judders inside her chest as she rows the final strokes toward the stranger. *I am being irresponsible*, she thinks. *How do I know this isn't all bullshit? Maybe he's a pirate. Or a rapist. How do I know this isn't a trap?* But her arms keep dipping the oars into the water, drawing her closer to him. She ties the dinghy to the rail of his boat, hands shaking. Standing up, she stumbles and nearly capsizes herself. "Oh, for goodness' sake," she says and grabs for his railing.

"Here," the stranger says. "Let me." He takes her arm gently, one hand at her elbow, the other gripping her palm. She feels his strength and also his hesitation. To him, lifting her onto the deck would be no more difficult than pulling up an anchor, but he lets her climb, braces her to keep her from sliding, saying quietly, "There we go. There we go." She believes him then, about the daughter. She believes he is a father.

"You came out of nowhere," she says once her feet are under her. Beneath her raincoat, sweat is rolling down her back. She is 58 and not in poor shape, but she's winded by the row and the climb over the railing and by her fear. *Why doesn't he have a ladder?* She looks around and takes in his boat's deck, which is worn but tidy.

She estimates the stranger to be twenty years her junior at least, maybe younger. He has a broad, open face, his forehead knotted in worry. For a moment he seems reluctant to invite her in, and it occurs to her that he has to trust her, too. She smiles and says, "I'm actually a nurse by training, so you lucked out." The words feel disorienting, coming out of her mouth, as if that life might be a story she once read, not her own past.

"Oh," he sighs. "Oh, thank you. Thank you for coming." He shakes his head, grips her hand in both of his in a gesture that surprises her so much she rocks back on her heels for a second. "She's in here," he says.

In the boat's cabin the cupboards and cushions are mismatched and the table's varnish worn to dullness, but the countertop has been wiped clean of crumbs and the stove's single burner polished bright. The lights Sonja saw across the water are warm, and there are quilts tucked here and there. It's a home.

The one off-putting detail is the stale odor of sickness. She recognizes it as flu from her days working in the hospital. Each illness has its own smell: Strep like fermentation. GI conditions tangy with acid. Flu is dry and stale and sometimes putrid-sweet like compost, the body working so hard to kill the virus that it begins to eat itself.

It crosses her mind that she herself could get sick, and that in an ideal situation she'd have a mask and gloves. But she'll have to make do without them. "Your girl, she has a fever?" Sonja asks.

The man nods, waves her toward the bow. He has to stoop under the low ceiling, but Sonja's head just grazes it.

He has put the daughter to bed on the V-berth beneath a quilt. She is little, maybe 5 or 6, and looks worse than Sonja imagined, the color in her cheeks flat, her face slack and a little doughy where it's swollen around her eyes and neck. *Lymph*, Sonja thinks. The fever must be high. Sonja puts her hand to the girl's forehead and estimates 104.

"She's been sick a few days," the man says. "But it wasn't so bad—just a cold. She's had so many colds, and"—he lifts his hands in a gesture she understands as confusion—"I thought she was getting better, and then in the night she went limp, suddenly. I'm out of acetaminophen and Gatorade and soup. And the fever won't go down."

"How many days?"

"Maybe four."

Four days? A decline that fast means the flu has likely turned into pneumonia. She says, "There's a hospital in Masset. Why didn't you just head for there?"

He looks pained. "The fuel," he says. He waves a hand toward the stern, and she remembers stepping over two red fuel containers.

A flare of anger. "You let yourself run dry up here?"

He straightens, squares his shoulders beneath his sweater. "They gave me bad fuel. Not in the line, but in the extra tanks. When I tried to use it, I realized—water in the diesel. I was stranded."

She remembers the stares she got in Moresby and Skidegate. They weren't keen on outsiders. "Fuckers," Sonja says.

"Yes."

"I'm sorry I assumed."

He looks her in the eye. "I'm a good father. I wouldn't harm my child."

Sonja nods. She's become jaded about people. She thinks of Melora looking inside all those strangers' chests in her small, dark ultrasound room, and of the way Melora said it doesn't matter that we're all the same on the inside; you could still never really know another person. Sonja heard it as a warning then: You can't trust anyone, not truly. At the time it suited Sonja to hear it that way. But now she sees she was wrong. Other people are usually clear about who they are; it's trusting yourself to read their signals correctly that is difficult.

"Give me a few minutes," she says.

She rows back to her boat, finds Tylenol and a thermometer, the jug of cider, a can of soup. She rows back. This time the muscles of her arms burn when she pulls herself aboard, but she manages it alone, bruising her knee as she stumbles over the rail. She rubs it, gets up. She hasn't felt such urgency about anything for so long.

In the tiny galley she gets to work finding a cup, a spoon. She crushes a pill to white dust, stirs it into the cider. In the V-berth the man lifts the girl into his arms and sits her against his chest. She's as loose as a rag doll, and Sonja turns away when, for an instant, memories flood her eyes.

"Okay," she says, sniffing and turning back. "Sooner the better." She takes the child's temperature. "As I thought," she says, "one hundred four." She directs the man to spoon cider into his daughter's mouth, then leaves the berth and finds a washcloth. Outside, she leans over the boat's railing and soaks the cloth in the cold seawater. The cool air outside is a relief. The stars are throbbing the way they do before they slide away at dawn. It's almost 4:00 a.m. She looks at the trees along the shoreline. *Stay away*, her internal voice says to the darkness. *Just stay away.*

Inside again she tells the man to put the cloth on the girl's chest, watches the little body shiver under it.

His expression is pained. "She's never been this sick," he says.

"We're doing what we can do."

Sonja thinks about her own boat, where she has a tank full of fuel, but she doesn't offer it. Not yet. Instead, she'll stay with him, see if they can bring the fever down. She gets up and makes the can of soup, puts a bowl on the little table, and tells the stranger to eat. "You don't have time to think of yourself when your child's sick."

"You're a mother," he says. "Only a parent knows this."

Sonja swallows the gravel that rises in her throat.

"Please eat with me," he says.

"No, but I'll sit, if that's okay." She takes the bench across from him. She can imagine the two of them sitting here together—this man and his girl. She can imagine the girl looking out the portlight at the water as he sailed them north. She wonders, *What was their tragedy? Where's the child's mother?*

"I didn't get your name," she says.

"Forgive me. It's Levan." He tips his head toward the berth. "And Natia."

Steam ribbons upward from the soup. She notices that he spoons outward, away from himself, and doesn't dip his face toward the bowl. Her grandmother would have approved of his manners.

"You're kind," he says. "Not everyone I've met out here has been."

She wants to say, *You don't know me*, but instead she says, "Tell me something about your girl."

He smiles. "She's a firecracker, you know?"

She nods. "Daughters usually are."

Angie ran away when she was 10. That was the first time. She waited until Sonja was at work on a Saturday and just walked out. The door was unlocked when Sonja came home, and for the first few hours both she and the police feared someone had broken in and taken Angie, but the following day Angie was spotted at the bus station in Everett. An officer drove her home in his cruiser. Child Protective Services investigated and eventually found

Sonja to be a responsible parent, though from then on, she had to pay a neighbor woman to sit in the house and watch TV during the hours Angie was home and she was on shift.

"Why'd you do it?" she asked her daughter.

Angie had no excuse, no reason. She was bored. She was tired of being on her own while Sonja was at work.

"Do you think I want to leave you here on your own? You think I'm at work because I'd rather be there?"

Angie eyed her. She had never been the sort of child to cry. Even as a baby she seemed to know the power of withholding. At nap time she'd stand in her crib, tiny and rigid, rather than lying down and submitting to her own fatigue. When Sonja settled her down on the mattress, she'd hold her body stiff as a rod. Now she hardened her jaw in the same way. The muscle below her ear tensed. "Good mothers don't have to leave their children," she said. Then, with a flash of fire in her voice, she added, "Good mothers don't get left."

Sonja held her temper. She didn't say, *Someday when you're a mother, you'll know what I've done for you.* She didn't say, *I didn't raise you to mouth off like that.* She didn't say, *The man who fathered you was no father, and I spared you that, at least.* And she didn't lunge forward and smack Angie across her face, which is what her grandmother would have done to her. She understood Angie just wanted to hurt her, as daughters will do, and she believed that was behind all the rest of it, too, in the years that followed—dropping out of school, vanishing, not calling for weeks on end. On and on the standoff went between them, each choosing her side and never wavering. And the more misbehavior Sonja ignored, the more Angie sought to punish her. That's how Sonja thought of it: punishment. Not for being a terrible parent, but for being incurious about her daughter, for being incapable of real interest. And what could she have done about that? We are who we are. She could not be a different person, a different woman, a different mother. That had been true when Angie was a stubborn baby and Sonja had finally just left her in the crib, turned out the light, and shut the bedroom door on her for the night; and it was true when she knew Angie was using and didn't put her in the car and take her to rehab, didn't stop her from living the way she was choosing to live.

"I always did the best I could for her, you know?" she'd told Melora, but even as she'd said it, she'd known it wasn't the whole truth.

Melora had squeezed her hand. "I'm sure you did, honey," she'd said. "I'm sure you did."

The clock mounted to Levan's wall says 5:00 a.m. Outside the water is softening to gray; the sky is beginning to bleach at its eastern rim. It will be light in half an hour, and Sonja will have to decide how long to wait with him for the girl's fever to break before she forces herself to be on her way.

"You spoke several languages," she says to Levan, and when he looks puzzled, she adds, "over the radio."

What he's told her about himself and the girl: He's 42, older than she first thought, though up close she noticed the wrinkles around his eyes and along his left cheek, where a dimple has become a deep crease. He has been on the water for six months and bought the boat in Vancouver. He's headed to Alaska, where there will be work, he hopes, in the fishing industry. He's Georgian by birth, has lived in Canada since 2013. She hasn't asked about the girl's mother, and he hasn't offered.

Sonja says that she speaks only English, though her grandmother, who raised her, tried to teach her other languages. "My grandmother spoke Swedish and Norwegian—learned at home—and English and French from school. A little German to accommodate her husband's parents, who came from Berlin during the First World War and still spoke it to each other," Sonja says. "When she was old, her mind began to move through time like it was a braid, not a line, and she slipped from one language to another."

"That's lovely," Levan says. "Time like a braid." He sips a cup of coffee—black, though he found a can of condensed milk for Sonja's when she requested cream and sugar. The drink is warm and soothing. She's missed sitting across from another person.

"I was a teacher," he tells her. "Secondary school. World languages. This was before." He tips his chin, indicating before the boat, this life now. Sonja understands. "But when I arrived in Canada, I became a jack-of-all-trades. So now, fishing. I know someone who says he will find me work." A smile. "We'll see how it goes."

"It's a shame, so much knowledge going unused."

"Not unused, just differently used, like your nursing."

"I chose to leave."

He meets her eyes. "So did I. Please don't feel sorry for me."

She sits back. "I didn't—"

"It's just that people say things—or they used to say things, before I came out here away from everyone. People assume I'm broken because of what my life has been. You see?"

She grips her mug, considers this. "Okay. I won't assume. You're out here with a child on your own, taking the slowest route to your destination, but I won't assume."

A flicker of amusement crosses his face. "I expected an apology."

She shrugs. "Why apologize? Everyone's broken, one way or another."

"You too, then?"

"Am I not someone?"

He nods. "You don't have to say. I knew when you showed me that gun."

"That's just sensible out here." She looks at him. "And no, I won't say."

Outside the portlight the sky is pale to the treetops. She gets up and goes to the boat's hatch, opens it so that a wash of cool air floods in, smelling of cedar and salt. There's birdsong. The glittering sound of water lapping the shore. She stands with one foot on the deck, the other inside. Her raincoat feels too hot. It's funny to her that she's kept it on, like the coat might be armor. Against what exactly, she doesn't really want to think about. She's been naked in the bed of more than one stranger out here on the water, but with this father and daughter, she has worn her coat despite its stuffiness. She can't live this way forever, she knows. She can't go on lonely and guarded for the rest of her life, no real connection ever again.

She forces herself to take off the coat, undoing the zipper and pulling at the sleeves. Her cheeks flame as she stands braless beneath her nightdress's thin cotton, wadding the coat into a ball in her arms. "I'm sorry. I'm too warm." Levan nods and looks away, a courtesy for which she's grateful. The air hits her, cold enough to raise goosebumps on her forearms and harden her nipples.

No one but Angie has ever seen her undone like this—matronly rather than sexy in her undress. Her hair a spiky mess around her head. Her body vinegared with dried sweat. She remembers the smell of her skin in the early days of parenthood—breast milk and yeast and acid. A mother musk. It could level her, the memory. That gravel in her has churned and churned tonight, and now it feels smooth and heavy enough to pull her to her knees. There's something not so awful about that after all this time.

She sits back down at the table and tells him, "I once nursed a child who had been mauled by dogs."

"Jesus."

"It was horrific, if I'm being honest, but I told the mother it could have been worse. I said that sort of thing all the time, to the loved ones."

"It was your job."

"Not really. I could have said nothing. Or I could have told them the truth. I knew that child wouldn't go home for weeks, and when she did, she'd be disfigured forever. But I said, 'It could be worse.'"

"That's true, though. She could have died. That would have been worse."

"Would it?"

He frowns. "I want my child alive, no matter what. I'd do anything to keep her alive."

"That's what we have to believe," Sonja says. "Mothers and fathers. We have to believe we've done the best for them, always."

The water pales with the sky, and the trees begin to pull in their sheets of shadow. The center of the bay is silver now, shining and opaque. Sonja feels a pulse behind her eyes, aches in her lower back and between her shoulder blades. She folds her arms around herself and says, "You haven't said why yet, but your girl has no mother." She means to be gentle, sympathetic, but it comes out like an accusation.

His expression is unreadable, and she thinks she's offended him with this obvious question so many hours into their conversation.

"Natia's mother lives in Toronto. She was not cut out for parenthood, and so she left us when Natia was only a few months old."

Sonja looks for grief but sees just fact. This has become his story. There's something amazing about that acceptance, and she envies it. "Don't you ever feel angry, though?" she asks. "Don't you ever feel cheated?"

A half smile. "Sure. Sometimes. That's life, isn't it? My anger is only for Natia now. The loss is really hers."

"She'll be fine, though. Children have a natural ability to forget. My grandmother raised me, and I never missed my mother. I wasn't scarred, the way people think."

"Maybe not a scar, but I think she is changed from who she might have been. It isn't natural to be motherless."

"No," Sonja says. She has to clear her throat to speak. "No, that's true enough."

"I'm sorry," he says.

"For what? For tonight? I'm glad to be helpful."

"No. For your losses. Whatever they might be."

She considers how to respond to this. It's well intentioned, not prying, but she still doesn't owe him anything. Instead, she says, "We should get some more fresh air in here," and she stands and moves through the little cabin opening all the portlights. A breeze slips in, and she stands for a long minute in the chill. She's shaking under her nightdress and hopes he doesn't notice. It's just a physical reaction to her fatigue, and it will pass.

"Let me make more coffee," Levan says.

"I should get back across the water." But as she's putting her coat on, the girl calls from the berth. Her voice is mewling, brittle with pain, and Levan lurches back to her, the boat swaying with his hurry.

Sonja gets the thermometer, wedges herself at the child's side, waits for the mercury to move. Beside her Levan is stone-faced, folded into himself, his arms crossed over his stomach as he rocks back and forth. Sonja rests her free hand on his knee. "She needs you to stay calm." She says this, but she remembers what it is to see your child hurting. Pain should retreat at love, but the truth is that love magnifies pain. No one likes to admit that, but she saw it plenty of times as a nurse: An old woman in her sickbed, her adult children leaning into each other with the shared ache. A man suddenly crying out, but the tears running down his wife's face. Pain can smell tenderness, she thinks. It's vicious and bottomless.

When she slides the thermometer from the girl's mouth and reads it, she considers the choices that open like a net in front of her: taking them to Masset herself and again being among people; calling for a medevac, a costly risk if the fever breaks on its own; or—the worst idea—waiting and hoping alone out here on the water. For a second she feels trapped in the knots of these impossible options. She decides to state only what is certain. "You and your girl need to get to Masset," she says.

He looks stricken. "But my fuel."

A second certainty: "You need to go now."

What she'd told Melora: She lost Angie through her own failures, her own misguided idea of how to love. Angie had been a good girl until she wasn't, and then everything she said and did and wanted seemed designed to hurt Sonja. She quit school when she was 17 and disappeared for a while. Sonja spent a winter driving between shelters and emergency rooms and churches, looking for her. And when Angie finally came home, just reappearing one day as if she'd always been planning to return, she was changed. She was skinny, her hipbones visible above the belt loops of her low-slung jeans. Her auburn hair had grown past her shoulders, and she wore it wavy and uncombed. She'd gotten a tattoo of a wolf on her left shoulder blade—the work of a guy she'd met at a festival in Missoula—and another, smaller one on her right lower back that she'd picked up from a tattoo artist she'd almost fallen in love with. She'd stayed on a co-op farm in southern Alberta for a few weeks, and then a friend's place in Denver, and then ridden along in another friend's van all the way back to the West Coast and north until she got home. She wasn't an addict, she said—she promised—but she'd tried things. Sonja felt a sick chill in her gut when she considered what that really meant. She could see the fire of it in Angie's eyes. She'd come home brighter somehow, a fuse set off deep in her, burning slow and hungry.

When Sonja had fallen pregnant—totally on her own and heavy with the burden of the decision she had to make about her future—she'd imagined the great terror of parenthood to be dullness: to feel one's keenness dulled by the boredom of being a mother, and then to raise a dull child, one not interested in the world around her, not curious enough to do more than choose a path and stay on it. Maybe that path would be a marriage, maybe a job. Dull comes in many shades of tedium. Sonja wanted her child to do better than that. Later her desire became more specific: She wanted Angie to do better than she herself had done. Wasn't that what a parent was supposed to want for their child? But maybe it had been a mistake to think like that.

"Why didn't you ever call me?" Sonja asked. "You must have known I was worried."

Angie scoffed, almost angry at this. "Jesus, Mom. How could anyone ever know what you're thinking?"

Sonja let Angie stay with her, but after a month she said there had to be rent. Angie was an adult, and it set a bad precedent to just let her loaf. It was for her own good. She meant for Angie to understand: The rent wasn't about money; it was about responsibility. She set it low—a couple of hundred dollars a month. Enough to nudge Angie into a job, but not enough to keep her from saving. She'd want her own place eventually, wouldn't she? She'd want to get on her feet, Sonja had suggested.

"What does that even mean to you?" Angie asked. She made air quotes, repeated it: "'Get on my feet?' You mean make the choices you would make."

"Do we have to battle over definitions now?"

"Fine. Fucking fine. I'll do whatever you want. There's more than one way to earn two hundred dollars."

She flashed her mother a look, and again that chill slid through Sonja, but she didn't take the bait. Instead, she got Angie a job at the hospital, serving coffee and doughnuts and sandwiches in the cafeteria while Sonja worked her regular nursing shift in the emergency room. It pleased her to stop in on her break for a cup of decaf and see Angie there, her hair tucked under the mushroom of the paper sanitary cap, her white apron tied in a neat bow at her waist. Now and then Angie could be convinced to take her break when Sonja did, and they sat together at one of the plastic tables, eating soft serve in wafer cones. It felt like progress, though Sonja couldn't say toward what exactly. Adulthood, maybe. Or peace between them. Either way this setup was safer than whatever Angie had chosen for herself in her time away. Sonja had shown her a safer, clearer path.

But by winter Angie was missing shifts. Sonja would go down for her break and discover Angie had never clocked in. She wouldn't come home for a night, two nights, and then she'd be back.

"What?" she said when Sonja questioned her. "I pay my rent. Am I under house arrest here?"

"No," Sonja said. "No, that's not it at all." And she let it drop.

It was February when the head nurse called Sonja into the break room, her expression tight in a way that Sonja recognized. The recognition unmoored her, and she didn't understand what was happening, even though later she thought she must have understood but rejected what she knew immediately.

The chaplain was also there, waiting for Sonja, and it was she who said it: Angie had died in the emergency room of another hospital, twenty miles north. An overdose. Accidental, they were sure.

The chaplain was a soft-bodied, middle-aged woman with bobbed hair and a pink twinset on over her clerical collar. She wore gardenia perfume, and the odor of it hung thick in the room. She reached across the table and took Sonja's hand, and Sonja thought how strange it was to hold another person's hand that wasn't Angie's. When Angie was a little girl, Sonja would hold on to her as they crossed downtown streets or made their way across the park to the swings. How out of body it felt to do it now, as if her hand were not her own but that other younger mother's still.

"I don't believe you," she said. But she was lying.

She drove alone to the hospital up north, insisted on seeing Angie's body, which looked just as the dead do, not at all like people in books say they do—*So lifelike*, or, *Just like she's sleeping*. No.

Sonja quit her job. She sold the condo where she and Angie had been living. She bought the boat.

That was a year and a half ago.

By midday Levan is gone, the tainted fuel washed from his line, replaced by her store of good fuel. It will get him to Masset, where the child will at least have a chance. If he hurries. If he's lucky. Sonja knows it's easy to be unlucky, to make a mistake.

Alone again on her boat, she fixes herself a bowl of canned chowder and a pot of coffee and takes her meal out to the deck. It's quiet, the sky cloudy and low. In a few minutes she'll find a radio station, one playing anything but talk, and by late afternoon her unease will start to rise, and she'll climb into her bed and wait for the day to end, the music sounding lightly, a distant companion.

"I'll come back with fuel. You won't be stuck here for long," Levan promised before he left. She could trust him, he said.

"It's fine," she told him. "Someone else will come along. You do for your girl."

"But you'll be stranded," he said. "You could be alone here for days."

"I know how to be alone."

He didn't understand. Most people don't. It isn't loneliness that breeds the dread. It's something else too complicated to explain. The way dusk can skin time and make its shapeless center suddenly visible. No one understands but people who have already seen that dark hole—people who are always holding the edge of it. Sometimes there's no redemption. Sometimes there is only that pit and one's fingers gripping as long as possible.

"Travel safe," Sonja told Levan.

As he motored away with the last of her fuel, she stood on her deck and waved. His wake curled after him for a few minutes, the reflections of the trees wobbling and shifting on the surface, threading into the ripples the breeze made. There was trickery in the way water filled and emptied, and the shadow he left quickly unraveled into nothing, just as she knew it would. As if he and Natia had never been there at all.

Outer Stars

That evening when he does not come home, Clara makes dinner for their daughter and carries on with their routines as if nothing is wrong. Outside, the city has not yet gone quiet. People are still returning from their final day of work. The street below their fifth-story window is still crowded with passing cars and bicycles. If there is something markedly different about the scene—unfamiliar or unsettling—she's not sure what it is, except maybe his absence. She feels it like a breath held—the waiting, a small pause in her body's rhythms, a pressure at the center of her chest that she knows will release the moment he walks through the door.

"R U OK?" she texts him.

"XO," he writes.

The whole night passes.

"Why isn't Dad home?" Moira asks over breakfast the next morning. The news is on the television, a woman in a red dress reporting before a digital background image of a sunny, blue sky. Out the window, the real sky is the color of cooked and cooling egg whites, soft and opaque. The reporter echoes what has been said and said over the last twenty-four hours, words like *particulate* and *aerosols* that might once have simply been terms but that are now panic invoking. They predict rain, which will clear it. Stay tuned for the full forecast. Clara turns it off.

Moira is 8. She looks like Clara, tawny hair and gray-brown eyes. Sometimes looking at her daughter is for Clara like seeing herself in a warped mirror. It's not the resemblance so much as a shadow of doubt or distrust—a feeling she's known all her life, and which her daughter, with all the love and attention she's been given as the only child of parents who desperately wanted her, certainly has no reason to feel. It's a feeling Clara would like to have spared her girl. Crack in a glass, snag in a cloth, knot of anxiety under the surface of every day. Little voice in her center whispering *nothing lasts*. Can you inherit uncertainty? It pains Clara to think she's passed it on, like a bad gene, this propensity for finding the dark hole of any moment.

She sets a bowl of cereal in front of Moira, the swim of bluish milk floating a sparkle of cinnamon and sugar crystals, and watches the girl stir before eating. With the first bite the concern on the child's face dissipates like clouds thinning. Moira tips the cereal bowl, drinks the sweet milk, and smiles, temporarily sated. She is elfin in the way of all not-yet-adolescent children—long limbed and big-headed. Cute and fragile and still in need of mother-love. Clara kisses her forehead, clears away the bowl. Moira gallops across the room, clambers up onto the couch, and cranes over to look out the window.

"When Dad gets home, we're going to build a model of the ship from *Outer Stars*," Moira says.

"Really?" Clara answers from the kitchen, just feet away. This apartment is small, efficient, but always enough for them. "Sounds like you two have a plan." Clara says it like it will be only hours. Like a sure thing.

"We do have a plan," the child says. "We'll play *Outer Stars*, then we'll *repticate* it." Moira grins, lifts her eyebrows—a new gesture, another mirror of one of Clara's own.

"Replicate it?" Clara asks, hoping Moira will correct herself.

"We're building it exactly. Exactly."

Outer Stars is a video game her husband and Moira play together on the weekends while Clara reads a book in the other room or goes out alone to walk where she will not be spoken to or needed. In the game, you—the player, but also the protagonist—have been sent into space following an undefined apocalyptic event that has made Earth uninhabitable. Space is your new landscape, in all its endless darkness, and your challenge is to make that darkness home. The darkness is not, however, vacant, or even actually dark; part of the challenge of the game is navigating the unexpected space flotsam—asteroids and meteoroids, comets, and planets with their circling moons. Once, Clara heard shouts of startled joy coming from the living room and rushed in to find that her husband and daughter had stumbled upon a nebula there on the screen, blue and neon pink and shot through with the diamond spangles of nascent stars. Beautiful. On the couch they had both dropped their controllers and were high fiving each other, beaming, explorers who had made their first big discovery.

Now, Moira presses her palm to the window. It's colder today than yesterday, and damp, and the glass clouds in a sweaty five-pointed fog around the print her hand leaves. "When will he be home?" she asks.

"Don't let's touch the windows, sweetheart," Clara says. "I just cleaned them." It's not true, but part of her worries about the dust coming in around the frame. The apartment is old, and the windows aren't weathertight. Another part of her worries—ridiculously—about Moira pushing hard enough to fall straight through the glass. She crosses the room and touches the girl's shoulder. "Go play in your room while Mama cleans up." It takes a moment of dallying on the couch, but Moira eventually clops off to her room, where in a moment there is the racket of Lego blocks spilling onto the rug. *God*, Clara thinks. *It's only 8:00 a.m.*

On a normal morning, her husband would be home. On a normal morning, the two of them would be walking Moira down the stairs, heading to school. They'd wear warm jackets today. Clara would pause on the stoop to help Moira zip hers, and then they would set off into this day. For an instant, she is swallowed by a wave of panic—not because such mornings were (are) the pulse of her life, but because in this new day, she doesn't know what happens next. *What comes next?* She stands in her kitchen, holding a dirty cereal bowl, a dirty spoon, and she cannot move. Her heart is a timer in her chest, counting down. She feels it clicking toward zero.

Eight o'clock is followed by nine o'clock she tells herself. *That's all.*

She repeats it, rolling the words like beads in her mind until the liquidity in her knees has gone solid and she can finish the breakfast cleanup, put things right again.

Before Moira was born, Clara and her husband moved to this city for a job. His job. He works as a nurse, her husband. His specialty is cardiac care. He trained at a hospital in Los Angeles, which is where she met him. She was a patient on his ward, her heart beating so slowly and so irregularly that she had to be admitted for tests, which eventually led to the surgery that replaced her malfunctioning mitral valve with a mechanical valve.

"Tell me about the surgery," she has often said to him, by which she means, *Tell me how you fell in love with me.*

It's not how he fell in love with her, of course—the surgery. But there is something about knowing that he was there when she was split open, her ribs cracked and her heart exposed, that feels like intimacy. He has seen her actual heart, and she likes the metaphor of that fact.

Is it normal to hear your pulse like someone's name whispered in your ear?

Is it normal to feel your chest ache when waiting for your beloved to appear at your door?

Is it normal to fall in love so soon after suffering a broken heart?

She wrote these sentimental questions in a journal she kept during the long weeks of recovery.

After they were married, she was glad for their unusual start. The silver lining of meeting your spouse under the worst of personal circumstances is that he's already seen you during the worst of personal circumstances. Who was she then? Someone feral. Someone just out of the deep woods. Someone with breath like animal musk and a gait like a lurching bear at the start of spring. Crisis reduces everything. Not *reduces* as in *makes smaller*, but as in *distills, intensifies what is essential to, thickens.*

Love was also a reduction—and therefore, maybe, a crisis. It was the self made richer and more complex. The world made deeper and more saturated. She had never understood this before him. The familial love she'd grown up with was scattershot, explosive and unpredictable. Too much free-floating need in the household for her to chart her own longing as a child in that broad constellation.

Like their own daughter, however, her husband was raised an only child, loved to the point of being treasured, which manifested in him a sense of complete assuredness that Clara still finds impossible, wonderful, confusing. Every Sunday evening his mother still calls him at five o'clock.

This close parent-child relationship is what her husband has re-created with their daughter. The games of *Outer Stars*, the way he stops into Moira's room when he comes home from his shift at the hospital each night at seven thirty, the album of photos of her on his phone—pictures that date all the way back to her birth. Moira is his center, his axis, just as he was his parents', just as he has been Clara's.

Is it normal to miss the arrhythmia? To miss the shadow beat after every regular one? To feel like the skip was where you were most alive? She wrote this in her recovery journal and later crossed it out. Who misses disorder?

Moira arrived as an accident and became a risk they decided to take. Clara's heart weathered it all—the love, the fear, the extra fifty-percent blood volume of pregnancy. *You're a hero*, her husband said to her at the birth. *No*, she thought: *I am a machine. I, with my mechanical heart.* Bone and titanium. Muscle and fabric. Electrical impulse and generation of cells. Pulse and pulse and pulse. A heart as reliable as a second hand, as the next breath taken, as the nightly moonrise. *I cannot fail.*

At noon she texts him again, then checks the news. The trains have stopped. The airports are closed. No rain yet. The advice of last night has still not altered: Do not attempt to drive unless absolutely necessary. Wear a mask when outdoors and change your clothes immediately upon entering your home. Inside the house, close your windows and shut vents to the outside, even chimney vents.

"Stay safe out there, folks," the reporter says. The camera shifts to a montage of images: an empty playground, a strip mall with closed signs on every shop door, a stand of alder trees nodding and tossing in the breeze. This last one is puzzling, unless it's there to conjure even more worry about what is being carried on the wind.

"Shut up," Clara says aloud, and turns off the TV. She thinks of the eighteenth- and nineteenth-century novels she's read in which fever travels by miasma, in which fog is dangerous. She thinks of Chernobyl. She thinks of Fukushima. Ruin carried on currents of wind, invisible, scentless, inescapable, inevitable.

In the bedroom, she finds a handful of old tights and leggings and walks through the apartment, stuffing the fabric around the window frames. She winds a pair of her husband's sweatpants into a snake of cloth and pushes it against the crack beneath the front door.

"What are you doing?" Moira asks. She is still in her pajamas, cotton pants and top striped like the rainbow. She looks like a Christmas card, like a catalog cutout.

God, Clara thinks. *What will I do?* But that's an anxious thought, anticipating a moment that isn't this one. She remembers that from therapy years ago: All you can control is your choices right now. "I'm just keeping us snug," she says.

Moira watches as Clara pinches the fabric tight into the crack. "Why are you keeping us snug?" she asks. "How will we get out of the house if the door is all jammed up like that?"

When she is grown, what will Moira remember of this time? Will it become, as so much of childhood does, diffused, all the blades and points rubbed off with time? Who knows. What does she, Clara, remember of the hardest parts of her own childhood? A recollection comes to her. She is sitting at her father's side on the couch in their suburban basement. On TV a bomb explodes. The bomb's cloud rises from the ground like a jellyfish made of fire and dust. It burns itself into Clara's brain, and for weeks she sees it when closes her eyes—cloud the shape of all her unnameable fears. Fear that threads her body with lines of heat, rattles her heart into an irregular beat, makes sweat break out on the back of her neck. At night it shakes her screaming from sleep. Her mother appears at the bedroom door, a frustrated expression on her face. She puts a cool hand against Clara's forehead, finds her without fever, and dismisses her. *It was nothing but a nightmare. Go back to sleep. Don't call me again.*

Clara has never said these words to her daughter. She wants Moira to understand that fear is as real as sickness. That loneliness can make a heart wear itself out. But who knows what shadow will follow her girl? Something. It's always something. And it probably won't be this—this time when the windows must be shut and her father hasn't come home to keep her safe, despite the bad air. She turns to Moira, smiles. "It's lunchtime," she says, and Moira bounds off to the kitchen for another meal—maybe they will blunt all of this with meals after all. It occurs to her that Moira remembering this day at all depends entirely on Moira surviving it.

"When will Daddy be home?" Moira says.

"Stop asking!" Clara says, too sharp, then sighs, softens her face and her voice. "Please stop asking, okay? Just please."

The girl's face crumples as if she's about to cry, but instead she runs to her room, where in a moment there is the narrow click of the door closing.

If there will be anything for Moira to remember, it will be this: the way her mother's voice could become a slap across the face, the way closing a door can so successfully separate the fragile need of your inner self from the certain disappointments of the outer world.

It is a little after two o'clock when a knock on the apartment door stirs Clara from the couch. She's fallen asleep, she realizes—or nearly, anyway. The image behind her eyes has been the setting of her daughter's video game: thick, velvet-black expanse glittered with stars and misty cloud veils of space dust. For an instant the knocking at the door is integrated into her half dream, disorienting and out of place. When she opens her eyes, the confusion is a web she has to wipe from her eyes, her mouth. She stands from the couch too quickly and her heart rackets in her chest. She stumbles against the couch, hits the leg of the coffee table, curses. Through her closed bedroom door Moira calls, "What is it? Are you okay? Is it Daddy?"

"It's not Daddy," Clara says. Her heart is a snag that keeps catching. The hot bruise on her shin pulses.

At the door she puts her eye to the circle of the peephole. No one is meant to be out, but here is this woman—angular and trench coated, her face obscured under a mask and sunglasses, her hair tucked inside a black felt cloche. She might have stepped out of some moment from the past, or from a fiction. Some thriller or detective movie. Someone else's fantasy.

"Can I help you?" Clara asks.

The woman's voice is muffled by the mask and the cloth Clara stuffed under the door.

"I can't hear you."

The woman repeats her string of sounds.

"It's not safe to be out, you know. You shouldn't be out."

Moira appears in the living room. "Who's here?"

"Go to your room." There must be more urgency in Clara's voice than she realizes, because the girl's eyes widen and she darts away.

On the other side of the door, the woman stands unmoving.

"If I let you in," Clara says, "you have to take off the coat and hat. And the shoes. Everything. Leave it in the hallway." She presses her face to the peephole again, watches the woman untie the sash at her waist, unbutton her coat and drop it in a heap. Next the hat. An uncoiling of dark hair falls to her shoulders. The mask she sets inside the crown of the upturned hat. She steps out of the shoes, looks at the peephole, and raises her hands. *Good?* Clara sees her mouth say.

She has never had this anxiety at the thought of opening her door to a visitor. The deliveryman from the Thai restaurant down the street, the mailman, the CSA woman who drops off their weekly bin of vegetables—they've all been in the apartment.

She toes the snake of fabric away from the door, opens it. A drift of cooler air washes in from the hallway and she holds her breath, gestures to the woman to come inside—quickly—and closes the door again behind her. The pile of coat and hat and shoes stays in a heap on the other side.

"Are you a neighbor?" Clara asks, though she already knows the answer.

"Can I sit?"

"I'm keeping the outside outside as much as I can," Clara says. "Precaution," she adds. "We have a child."

Shift in the woman's expression—maybe regret, Clara thinks. "I understand," the woman says. "I just felt you should know that he's safe. He's at work now, of course—it's the middle of the day. But last night—. We decided it was safer for him to just stay." She turns her eyes away from Clara's. "I wanted to tell you he is safe."

"Oh," Clara says.

"I wouldn't have come—I know it violates the agreement—but because of everything . . ." The woman points to the bank of windows on the far wall, and Clara pivots to look—stupidly, she thinks even as she does it, as if an explanation for anything might be there, hanging like a dropped moon from the branches of the trees. As if she might be able to look out the window and say, as if any of it makes sense, *Oh, of course. The world is upside down. I forgot, but now I understand.*

The woman is not what Clara has imagined. She is short, not tall. Severely thin rather than soft. She is somewhere later in midlife than Clara herself, her dark hair veined in gray and her bare face lined at the eyes and around her wide mouth. She wears a black sweater and black tights, the only bright thing about her a cropped corduroy skirt the color of an egg yolk. In her stocking feet she looks tiny. So short and petite, she could be mistaken for a girl from a distance, and what should Clara make of that? What should she make of that?

"Why didn't he call me?" Clara asks. "He should've just called."

The woman's face softens into something like a smile. "He left his phone at our place this morning. On the counter. He must have set it down when he made his breakfast." She rolls her eyes, grins as if she's sharing a welcome intimacy, an inside joke between them, the two women who divide his love. "You know him," she says. "He can be forgetful." She withdraws his phone from her pocket and hands it to Clara. In Clara's hand the square glass face and plastic body of the thing are warm with the woman's heat.

Suddenly, Clara's angry. Her anger is an explosion under her skin. When she opens her mouth, smoke will billow off her tongue. She says, "The agreement is that I will never have to see you."

The woman touches her own chest as if Clara has struck her there. "I'm just telling you he's safe. It's an emergency. That changes everything." A small sigh. "He tells me you worry."

He tells you? "No," Clara says. She could rage, but she keeps her voice steady, aware of Moira in the other room. Still, she shakes as she speaks. "There is us, and there is you. Two separate worlds. And now you're here where you should never be. You need to leave." Tentacles of anger unfurl and constrict around Clara's throat, which aches to yell—to scream. "We have a child here," she says again. "You need to leave."

"I knew it was a risk to come," the woman says. Again, the gesture toward the windows.

Later Clara will turn this sentence over and over again in her head, as if it is a Rubik's Cube whose pattern she must crack before she can set it down. Does the woman mean that it was a risk to come here, specifically, to this apartment where Clara and Moira are cloistered and waiting? Or does she mean that it was a risk to be out in the air at all right now—a risk to her, to the woman herself, and to her wellness? Does she mean that she has performed an act of personal sacrifice to come here? Or does she mean that her coming here puts at risk Clara's well-being, peace of mind, family stability, already-broken heart?

Clara's heart is steady, though. Standing in the empty few feet of space between the couch where she was just lying and the door she has just opened, she closes her eyes and listens for her pulse and finds it regular. She touches her fingers to the dip at the base of her throat, little well where her heartbeat usually gasps up to the surface like a carp to the water's rim, but her pulse is clear and even.

"I knew you would be worried," the woman says. "In your place I would have been worried. He said you were worried."

"He shouldn't have said anything to you about me."

"Look, this is a courtesy. Because we're—you know, with our arrangement—a kind of family."

"No," Clara says. "No."

"I don't mean to overstep."

"Never come here."

"I'll go, then."

"Now."

The woman hesitates, twists her body like a question mark on the point of one of her sock feet. "If it were me, I would have worried," she says. "If this had happened on a night he was with you instead, I would have worried. I meant to be empathetic." She lets out a long breath, shakes her head.

Clara grips the doorknob. "I wouldn't come to you," Clara says. "You do not exist. I will never come to you."

The woman nods, leaves. Clara closes and locks the door behind her and stuffs the fabric back into the space beneath it.

What do you want? he said. *When you think of our future, what do you want?*

This was before Moira, when they were just beginning to imagine their lives together. (Two cartographers, he had called them, mapping the wide, dark, open sea that lay ahead. When she'd told him there was no map for the deep waters, he'd only laughed.)

"Future" is such an ambiguous word, she said, though. *It assumes we know anything about tomorrow or the next day. It assumes we get to choose.*

You're afraid to be truly happy. That's the trouble. You're always waiting for the end. A tease in his tone, a half joke that half stung.

And you, she said, *you've never been denied anything. That's your trouble.* She said it, but she kissed him. Sweet man. Sweet boy. What would she lose if she lost him? She couldn't map that either.

Clara, he said. *We're making our own world now. It doesn't have to look like anyone else's.*

Fine, she said. *My world is here, us. I want us and us and us and us and us and us, on repeat, until I'm dust. And whatever else you need to find out there, go have it, but I don't want to know. Here, it's us.*

Clara—

No. That's my agreement. I'll never ask, and I don't want to know. But here, nothing changes, nothing gets messy.

That's not an agreement, that's a concession.

She shook her head. *It's what matters to me*, she said, and part of her was surprised to hear those words come from her mouth.

The afternoon burns on. Moira emerges from her room with an armful of books, which Clara reads to her, the two of them curled into each other on the couch, and when that is done, the girl asks for *Outer Stars*, and because Clara is tired—too tired, honestly—she says yes. Fine. They can play *Outer Stars.*

"I'll teach you, Mama." Moira leaps from the couch to grab the remotes. The TV screen illuminates.

Outside, the light is going thick with late day. Custard colored for an hour, then the pale near-green shade of gray that could mean rain. The growing dusk makes visible the lights in the apartment windows across the street, creamy yellow squares. Typically, Clara loves this time of day, when the workers of the world begin to return home. She loves the way the hard carapaces of the buildings seem to soften and crack open as the home lights behind the windows come on. Here, a family sitting down to dinner. Here, a woman on the telephone. Here, a child leaning over his homework, glowing ball of the dining room's pendant lamp hanging like a moon above his head. Good night. Tuck in. Everything you had to do today is behind you.

Tonight, what becomes visible is just existing light—light that's been there all day, there but invisible against the daylight's glare. Like her, everyone has been home, stuck in, waiting. The city a single body breathing and heart beating. She watches a man in an apartment across the street approach his window and stand, looking out. Is he also waiting for someone to come home? She has never thought so much about waiting—not even when she was in the hospital, not even when she was expecting Moira. Those pauses, however, were different in that they had positive endpoints. Definite conclusions. And in both cases she was the epicenter of her own crisis or joy—all risk existed within the confined space of her own body. Now, what control does she have over anything that might come next—or not come? That knock at the door was the knife that cut her loose from her tether to everything she planned to expect, and now she is a body floating, unmoored.

"This is the planet Daddy and I are trying to cultivate," Moira says, interrupting Clara's thoughts.

On the screen a luminescent purple sphere rotates one way and then the other, depending on the buttons Moira pushes on her controller. She zooms in and Clara sees more closely the surface of the planet—soft, granular. "Can you walk on it?" she asks, and Moira clicks and clicks until plumes of soil rise.

"It's our feet doing that. There's no water here. It's why Daddy and I haven't figured out how to grow anything yet."

"What would you grow?"

"There are plants you can earn with your points. Space plants. They don't need air. They have no roots, so it's fine that the soil is so sooty. But, still, you need water."

"*Sooty*?"

"Like ashes. You know."

The girl's eyes are wide, hyperfocused and unblinking. She jostles her thumbs on the mini joysticks of the controller, manipulates their character off the surface of the purple planet again and up, into the lift of dark space.

"Why can't I see our body?" Clara asks. "Our character's body."

"It's first person, Mom. Duh."

"That was sassy. I don't like sassy."

"Sorry." The girl frowns, turns her face to Clara. "Sorry."

Clara kisses her forehead.

"Look," the girl says. "Here's our foot, see?" She clicks and a gray moon boot appears at the lower edge of the screen. "Here's our hand." Another click. A thick glove, articulated fingers that open and close. "You just don't get a face. You're just another person. But in space."

"Right," Clara says.

On the screen, as their character drifts forward, new planets come into view in the distance. A green orb spinning inside several rings, halos of gritty debris. A massive orange ball with a surface that roils and churns like bile. There are chunks of rock, bits of unidentifiable space junk just floating. And then, what Moira's been searching out: a nebula—her favorite feature of the game. It explodes onto the screen, and Moira shrieks with delight. It is pink and green and blue and yellow. Feathers of ink spinning out in a glass of water. Rainbows of oil marbling a puddle. Synapses firing in a branching dance on a brain scan.

"It's beautiful," Clara says.

"I think so," Moira says. "Do you know that a nebula is a real thing?"

"I do."

"Daddy told me. It's a cloud of stuff that clings together. Sometimes the cloud gets so heavy, it smashes itself. That's how new stars are made." Moira nods, licks her lips, her eyes fixed on the screen.

Clara watches the nebula open and open as Moira directs their character forward. It is peony blossom and desert landscape. It is the jeweled inside of a geode and the liquid center of the ocean both, at once.

"Wow," Clara says.

"Yeah, I know." Moira smiles. "It's so pretty, I forget until I remember again."

On the screen the nebula spires and curves, then dissolves into grains of beautiful, royal blue dust.

She has just put Moira into the bathtub when she hears his key in the lock. At the door she kicks away the snake of fabric. “Nothing from outside comes in,” she says to him first. She steps away while he strips off his coat and shoes, his scrubs, the N95 he’s worn home over his face. These things he knots into a single wad of clothes, and she brings him a trash bag, where he deposits them to be taken to the wash.

In his shorts he is himself again—not the stranger she’s been mourning all day, but just himself, her husband. She wants to step forward into his chest, feel the warmth of his skin against her cheek, but she resists that impulse, knots the trash bag.

“There’s food, if you want it. Moira and I ate. But shower first, right?”

“I know she stopped by,” he says.

“Moira’s in the bath.”

“She’s fine for a few minutes there. Talk to me.” He is nearly naked and still standing on the narrow rug at the door.

“What?” Clara says. “What do you need to say?” She faces him, holds the trash bag away from herself.

“I made the choice I thought was safest,” he says. “They were saying not to go out in it. Not to be outside.”

“But you managed tonight. You’re here now.”

“I am.”

“Then don’t lie to me. You made a choice. You broke the agreement, letting her come here.”

"I didn't *let* her do anything. She came all on her own. It was bound to happen. I don't understand your anger."

Heat flares behind her breastbone. How can she explain to him that the woman is a crack in the glass, a hole through which all the air will escape? How can she tell him that it's as if he's broken all the windows and the dark is rushing in? "You should have insisted she stay away. Now she's been here. In our house."

He looks remorseful. She recognizes the expression on his face—boyish, regretful. She's seen it before, and in spite of herself it has been what has brought her back to him.

"I told you, she came on her own. Her decision, not my request."

"I never want to see her. I never want her to see us. She's not part of this family. She's nothing to us."

"Look," he says. "I love you, and I love Moira. We're a family, here. That will not change."

She wants to say, *Did you make a mistake when you chose me?* She wants to know if when he looks at her, he still sees her cracked open, heart exposed, and if that is why he cannot step away.

"I know you love our family," she says instead. "I do know that."

From the bathroom come the sounds of splashing, the drain's soft glug. "Daddy?" Moira calls. "Do I hear Daddy?"

"Get your PJs on and we can read a bedtime story!" he calls to her, his voice all joy.

"Daddy-daddy-daddy-dad!" Moira yelps. She is in the kitchen then, towel lopsided around her tiny body, hair dripping fat wet splots on the floor.

"Pause!" Clara stops the girl. "Daddy has to rinse off first."

He grins, does a goofy dance in place that makes Moira shriek with laughter from her puddle across the room. "Go on now," he says. "Let Mom help you while I clean myself up."

Clara drops the trash bag and gathers Moira in her arms, scoops her into a ball of leg and arm and towel fold, carries her away. From the bedroom, she hears his feet on the floor, the bathroom door closing, the shower fitzing on. Like any night. Like normal. It infuriates her.

Soon, Moira is dried and swaddled in fleece pajamas and snuggled onto the couch. He emerges from the shower clean, hair still damp and curling at the nape of his neck. Moira is all delight, all luminescent daughter-child in his presence, incandescing for him and he for her. How she adores him. How he needs to be adored by her. *The two of them*, Clara thinks. They make their own light together, Moira and her father, and outside the circle of that light, Clara can step away more easily.

She is just thinking this when at the window, finally, there's the *tick tick tick* of rain. Slow and thin, then thick and heavy drops that streak the windows, gliss the black branches of the trees.

"Rain!" Moira shouts.

Clara turns on the TV. A feed runs at the bottom of the screen, declaring the "all clear." The storm has blown it out east, away from the city. The rain has cleared the air. It's safe again. For now.

"Oh, I love rain," Moira says.

Her father laughs. "Let's smell the rain," he says, happy. They jump up from the couch and start the work of clearing away the cloth Clara has stuffed along the sills.

Clara leaves them together and gets her coat, her umbrella. "I'm walking," she says from the door.

"This late?" He turns to her. "It's dark."

"I'm walking," she repeats, and before he can say anything more, she is out of the apartment, down the elevator, through the glass doors of the lobby, and onto the wet and glittering street.

She is mostly alone. The streetlamps are on, and she moves between their spheres of light. The rain on her umbrella pits an even rhythm, smells stiff and mineralized—a good smell that makes her think of childhood swims in summer lakes and of her own body after a hard run in the days before her heart surgery. *What would her life have been if hers had been a normal heart?* she asks herself. If every beat didn't leave its shadow behind it? She pictures her *Outer Stars* avatar moving across the sooty soil of the screen.

A body is just another kind of sea, isn't it? Where earth and atmosphere meet and mix—another unpredictable, liminal space. She wonders now how she could have expected herself to be the certain one. How she could have thought she'd never change her mind.

She makes it all the way to the piers before she stops. There's a crowd gathered, and she's startled. People in rain slickers and baseball caps and ponchos made of Hefty bags stand shoulder to shoulder at the pier's railing, fishing poles extended and lines let loose into the water below.

"What is this? What's happening here?" she asks a man in a rain suit, bright yellow hood pulled up over his head.

He turns from his pole. "Squid," he says.

Here and there, rowboats. And from each boat a lantern on a cord, dropped into the sea and casting a halo. In the centers of these otherworldly, milky, ultramarine rounds of light, the boats sit tranquil, just drifting, while all around them, lit visible, the bodies of tiny schooling fish form flashing bands of silver.

"The lights are for you?" Clara asks. "Up here on the pier? So you can see into the water?"

The man shakes his head. "For the squid. Attracts them." He nudges a five-gallon bucket at his feet, and Clara peers inside at a swim of the white, fleshy tubes: squid. So many of them bobbing there in a few inches of water, just enough to keep them alive.

"I never knew they like light. Why?" she asks. "Why when it's going to kill them to follow it?"

The man shrugs. "No one knows. They like it because they like it." He's done talking to her.

"Right," she says.

When she gets home, she'll tell Moira about the squid. She'll say, *Did you know a squid has three hearts?* This is a fact—the only one she knows about squid.

Revision

The rest of Paris is still asleep when they leave the hotel. Outside, Ilse loops a scarf around her neck against the cold and upturns the collar of her coat. It is January, the day before her 64th birthday, and the air is damp and chill and still liquid blue with night. No one's lights are on in the apartments lining the street, the faded shutters all closed behind the iron grilles of the upper-floor balconies and the curtains drawn across the windows of the lower floors. Ilse hurries to tug on the hat she'd stuffed into her bag, to tuck the fringe of the scarf into the flaps of her coat, careful to watch her footing on the cobblestones and to sidestep the French refuse—wet receipt paper and cigarette butts wind-washed in clusters toward the gutters, the occasional pile of frozen dog shit.

"Hold on," she says to the man she's traveling with—Joel—who is a few paces ahead. "You're walking so fast.

We won't miss it. God knows, everybody sane is still in bed." He turns, and a look she hasn't seen on a man since the last years of her marriage crosses his face. *I'm weary*, she remembers her ex-husband saying when she questioned this expression in the months before their divorce. *I'm just weary*. But, of course, that was always a lie. Fatigue, she's come to understand, is not the same as regret.

They pass another block of apartments, a row of darkened shops—*Fermé*, the signs all say. The streets are empty of everything but a parked motor scooter here or there, leaning at the usual petulant angle toward the sidewalk; a knotted plastic sack of someone's dinner trash; an orange cat cupped into the stone elbow of a bookstore's vestibule, fur puffed against the weather. Thirty years ago, when she was first here with her husband and two young children, they'd come in the summer—June—so that Otto could teach a study-abroad course, and the city then was a lush racket of color. The pale blue and pink and gold ornamental bric-a-brac of Belle Époque architecture. Stoops cluttered with terra cotta pots spilling herbs. Window box gardens bursting geraniums the startling florescent red of she-didn't-know-what. It was all exactly as she'd envisioned Paris since she'd first wanted to go as a 16 year old sitting in a high school French class.

This trip, however, has been a series of disillusionments. How she'd never imagined that winter must come here, too—that Paris must go naked and gray in January, just like home—she has no idea, but there it is. The chill and the ice-edged fog and this low, smoke-blue sky of near-dawn are shocks, shadows, when she arrived expecting light (and, god, doesn't she always?).

Ilse pauses at the front window of a café, the only open place she's seen. "Should we get a coffee?" she asks.

Ahead of her on the sidewalk, Joel pauses, hesitates, looks at his watch. "We can't be late."

"Just a coffee. It'll be quick," Ilse says. "Oh," she breathes. "Smell that?" A draft of coffee-carameled air has wisped out through the building's vents to where they stand.

Joel's sigh appears as a physical cloud. He looks at his watch. "It's never just a coffee here. It's an hour, at best. The concierge said not to miss the first train." The next one will be crowded, he explains, and the one after that worse. Missing this one will set back the whole excursion. They'll spend the day neck-and-neck with tourists. He hates tourists.

Ilse only half listens to this. There have been moments when she's wondered what possessed her to invite Joel along on her trip. Alone, she might have stayed in the center of Paris instead of on the economical fringe; she might have spent a whole day unapologetically wandering the treed, gravel paths of the Louvre's garden without ever having set foot inside the museum; and she most certainly would right now be downing a cup of coffee and not thinking a goddamned thing about the train schedule. But, also, she knows why he is here: He is a stay against loneliness. That much, at least, she has gleaned from the week they've spent together. And though she's still uncertain what to make of that recognition, she doesn't feel guilty. Who would want to be lonely in Paris?

Joel withdraws the map from his back pocket—two pages he's torn from the guidebook and stapled together at the center so that the whole of Paris might be spread out on one sheet, the city a pink swell like a misshapen heart in a sea of blue and green. "One more block," he says. He closes the map again. "Let's just get there so we can relax. We don't want to fight the crowd all day, do we?"

"No," Ilse says. "No, I don't want to fight anything."

"Great." He turns. "Once we're there, I promise, you can eat all you want."

She lets this last bit slide, hitches her bag over her shoulder, and follows him.

The truth is that Joel is a kind man, usually. He's a former engineer, and his online dating profile noted his preferences as nonfiction, road biking, spaghetti Bolognese, and travel. On their first date he asked to meet her for lunch rather than dinner. Over a Cobb salad, he told her that he'd worked for Boeing for thirty-five years exactly; the date of his retirement at age 62 was calculated to leave him a modest living and a good number of healthy remaining years to spend doing what he hadn't had time for as a younger man—*hiking, cooking lessons, maybe marriage.* This was September. By October they'd been on three more dates—drinks at a jazz club, a midday walk around the university's arboretum, a steak dinner at a swanky new restaurant overlooking the bay. She learned that he'd been honest about everything on his dating site profile, and that he, like her ex-husband Otto, was a man who spent far more time in his head than in his body. This gave her pause. She wasn't the sort of person who needed the same lesson twice. She'd spent two years in counseling after the divorce, mucking about in the emotional septic tank of her marriage, and she'd come out of it knowing two things for certain: (1) she would never marry again, and (2) she would still occasionally like a man to take her to dinner on a Friday night, and also maybe sometimes to bed, but that was it.

In the end, though, Joel was not at all like Otto. Where Otto had been distracted, dreamy, Joel was meticulous and sober. When Otto slipped into his head, it was always as if he'd gone into another world, all his own, from which she was excluded, even after nearly forty years by his side. Joel's thoughts, on the other hand, were wholly of this world—facts and numbers, details and data. He was smart, clearly—she'd known that about him right away—and he had a memory unlike anyone else she'd ever met. Charmingly, he could still recite poems by Poe and Frost that he'd been made to memorize as a child, and he knew the batting average of every Minnesota Twins hitter since 1961. Planes were his polestar, however. Each time a plane broke the clouds overhead, Joel could look up and name it: *Boeing 737-500, Learjet, Cessna 172 Skyhawk.* His ear had archived their sounds. He could envision their mechanics, too—jets the size of cruise liners, each engine half the weight of an elephant, and he could, one-two-three, as simply as fitting together a child's puzzle, explain the intricate joining and arrangement of every part.

"How do you do that?" Ilse had asked the first time he'd demonstrated this parlor trick for her. They were out walking the wide path around the lake near her condo when a plane's roar cut through the quiet. She waited while Joel followed its path across the blue sky. On the ground the autumn trees were already tipped in red, about to flame, and the air was static with the change in season. Joel had spent the night at Ilse's—not for the first time, but for the first time with sex rather than just dinner and a late movie and an offer to sleep on her couch. And though he wasn't the first man in the five years since Otto, and though he was entirely unsurprising as a lover (the whole endeavor—because that seemed the fitting word—performed as neatly and to everyone's satisfaction as if he'd read a set of directions beforehand), she was pleased to have climbed that peak, so to speak, and to now have it behind them, so they could get on about the business of knowing each other.

The plane's thunder petered out.

"Sounds like a Cessna," Joel said.

"Do you do birdcalls, too?" Ilse joked.

"One of my many useless talents."

"Don't be so humble. It's impressive."

He shrugged. "Every guy in my office would have known that plane. We were paid to know." He pointed at the blue vacancy overhead. "It was my life's work. There's never been anything else for me."

"But you're retired now."

A look of unmistakable grief crossed his face. "True."

"And retirement hasn't been all you thought it'd be?"

Joel shook his head. "That's not it exactly, but I do miss the routine of a job. I miss the daily tasks, the to-do lists, all of that. The clear reason to get up and get going every morning."

He'd worn close-fitting nylon jogging pants, a high-end windbreaker, orange running shoes. It was the wardrobe of an old man trying to look younger. He looked sheepish admitting to a lack of purpose.

"I can't say I feel the same," Ilse said. "But, then again, my routines weren't especially exhilarating. You can't imagine how many hours of my life I've spent wiping up people's bodily fluids and replacing empty toilet paper rolls." She'd told him already that she'd been a nurse, a mother, a housewife, but she hadn't yet confessed the lingering resentment about much of that work. She didn't want to seem boring, whiny, tedious. She didn't want to remind him too often that he was dating a woman with grown children—a woman with grandchildren.

But his expression eased. "They were lucky to have you, your family."

"Well."

"Honestly." He leaned to kiss her. "If only I'd met you sooner in life."

It was saccharine, sentimental. He didn't have Otto's romantic originality, but, then, where had that gotten her with Otto in the long run? What was the show really worth in the end? She'd much rather go a different route now. And, anyhow, the predictability of a man's romantic gestures did not necessarily indicate the depth of his feelings.

She stepped nearer and let Joel catch her hand and hold it, his palm warm against hers as they walked. It was a dry and beautiful Saturday—something scarce in their little northwestern corner of the country in the fall—and she thought, *I'm happy. Good grief, am I happy! Am I really happy?*

"You know, I was scared to retire, actually, because work was everything for so long. When I retired, it was like learning how to be human." He laughed. "I'd never tried that before. I'd always just been an engineer."

"I wonder about what it's like for convicted prisoners when they've finally served their long sentence and are let out. They go in at 18, say, and come out at 70. All of their middle years have been spent as a person they can no longer be. And now they're old."

"I liked my work. It wasn't a mistake to devote myself to it."

"Oh no, I don't mean that. I mean, we all make mistakes. We all waste the time we have."

"I don't feel that way."

"How can you not feel that? It's not something you can agree or disagree with. It's fact. We all make mistakes." Ilse felt the old rise of excitement—the hackles prickling—that preceded a good discussion—something she did miss about living with Otto. They could always have it out about an idea and then slip right back into the day, not a ruffle left between them.

Joel went quiet, though. "I gave you my point of view. I don't want to argue with you."

It seemed a contentious thing to say, and Ilse waited, feeling chastised, to see if this was to be the start of their first fight, but he pointed to a bench along the path, and they sat. Before them the black lake was skimmed in reflected light. The light swam and pooled and broke with the movement of the water, reassembling again an instant later.

"Okay," she said. "Is this how you disagree with people? You clam up?" She took two clementines from the pocket of her jacket and handed him one. "Maybe I'm being too direct, but you should know now that I'm generally too direct." With her thumbnail she split the skin of her own and slipped a section into her mouth, the tang sharp and immediate, bright as this bright day. "I'm not saying I'm too old to change, but I am too old to pretend I'll change."

Joel smiled at this. "No, don't change. You struck a nerve, I guess. I made plans and then I lived them. More or less. That's probably the mistake, for me, if there is one. I didn't waste time, but I was perhaps too determined not to waste it." He laid his hand on her thigh.

Again, she thought of Otto, and of how he would have responded to this confession. *Chaos births life, but order births only habit*, she'd heard him tell a student more than once. It was a borrowed phrase, and a botched one, too. He'd read it in some book and couldn't remember the exact wording. Still, it was poetic, this philosophy. The world in constant, wild turbulence. Beauty and love and loss all unchartable. Our bodies a wonderful anarchy. Our lives impossible to map. The students loved it. They swooned. Especially the young ones, who wanted nothing more than an adult to validate their impulses, to confirm that, sure enough, the instability they were living was a kind of authenticity. It was such a buzzword for a while—*authenticity*. She'd hated it. *I am my authentic self.* As if you could ever be anyone else.

Although, she thought now, maybe you could be.

Ilse shifted to face Joel. How different he was! How interesting to think about what her life might have been like with him instead of with Otto. How interesting to think about who she—as his wife—might have turned out to be.

An idea materialized in her mind, and before she could stop herself, she was speaking. "I'm planning a trip," she said. "For my birthday. If you like, we could plan it together."

Within the day Joel had found a reasonably priced hotel in the 17 ème arrondissement and booked them a red-eye.

On the train they do not speak. Joel reads a crime novel on his tablet. Ilse keeps her eyes on the window. She wonders whether he's avoiding conversation with her, or if, perhaps, they've just exhausted all conversation in the two weeks they've spent together here in France. This, she's come to see, is one difference in the life she would have led with Joel versus the one she did live with Otto: With Joel there would have been much more silence. At a certain point in her life, when the children were small and every day was filled to overflowing with riotous noise, she would have relished such quiet, but that point has passed.

She watches the commuters board and take their seats, their faces chapped pink at the cheekbones and chin from the chill outside, their expressions stiff. This is their routine. They are headed to offices and computer screens, a morning spent looking out a window at the gray sky. She reminds herself that she is on vacation. That this is luxury. That she is sitting on a train with nothing she must do or say or think. Honestly, the silence is good. Sitting in comradely silence with another person can be good.

"I've been on this train before," she says.

He raises his eyes from his reading to look at her.

"When we were here all those years ago—Otto and I, with the children," she continues. "I don't remember much of it."

Joel makes an expression that is akin to shrugging with his face: a lift of the eyebrows, a pursing of the lips. It's the look he gives her when she's said something of little to no interest to him. She knows this, but she goes on anyhow.

"It must have been uneventful if I've forgotten it. The children must have been well-behaved—no one motion sick or tantruming." She taps the window glass with a finger. The gray-brown buildings that rind the city swim by, one indistinguishable from the next. Her mind flurries, flips through the mental slides she's held on to from that trip, trying to remember. "Sylvie was probably just about 6, and Anders almost 2, I think, so it seems impossible that they would both have been good sitting here with nothing to do."

"Maybe they slept," he says.

"You've never traveled with children."

"That child's sleeping." Joel directs her gaze to a little boy lying across a woman's lap on the other side of the aisle. "It's the motion of the train, like a rocking chair. They've done studies. The motion synchronizes the brain waves. It's lulling." He fishes in his coat pocket and comes up with a nest of wound wire, his earbuds. "I'm going to listen to this, if you don't mind. I downloaded an audio history of the palace. If I listen now, it'll save time in walking through the exhibits." He smiles, plugs himself in.

Ilse folds her hands in her lap. There's no point in trying to talk him into conversation. When she envisioned them together on this trip, she saw long hours of walking arm-in-arm along the Seine, days of deep afternoons filled with discussions over café tables and glasses of wine. For years she and Otto had planned to come back to France someday, when the children were grown and they could go alone, free to take their time in traveling and to think only of themselves. They would linger in the Luxembourg Garden, which they'd rushed through all those years ago because the children had wanted only to ride the carousel and sail toy boats on the pond. They would eat an actual meal in an actual restaurant. They would stay awake late into the night, picking each other's brains in the heated, wandering way they had before their children were born. This, of course, all planned before Otto decided he wanted out of their marriage, before he left her. No matter. It was a dream, anyway, and she supposes she never revised it to account for Joel's presence instead of Otto's, and for the differences in their temperaments.

She pats Joel's knee placidly and scans the train car for interest. Several other people have put on earphones. An old woman near the back has spread the leaves of a newspaper over two seats and is reading with a magnifying glass. A teenager just ahead of her is performing careful surgery on a pomegranate. And across the aisle, the child Joel pointed out is still asleep. His mother has a book open and braced against the seat in front of her. With her free hand, she strokes the boy's hair. The child is 4, 5 at the most. His legs are long, and his feet hang off the end of the seat, big in their sneakers. He's still young enough that his face looks babyish in sleep, his mouth slack, his eyelids full and purpled and lined in thick lashes. The mother's arm cradles his head. Ilse remembers holding her son in just this way, touching the warm spot at his temple where his pulse flickered. Occasionally her youngest grandson will still let Ilse hold him like this, though even he is getting too old to be cradled now.

She is recalling this—the weight and warmth of her own babies and grandbabies in her arms—when the man in the row behind the mother and child folds his magazine and leans forward. "Excusez-moi," he says. He pushes his knees against the back of the woman's seat.

"Pardon," the woman says. She is perturbed. She covers her son's ear with the cup of her hand. The noise of the train is a rhythmic whoosh.

The man leans nearer, puts his mouth to her ear, and whispers something.

Perhaps he is familiar to her? The boy's father, maybe, Ilse thinks. But no. Something nearly imperceptible has hardened in the woman's face, like a skin of ice forming on the surface of a lake.

The man has a short, dark beard that reminds Ilse of her son's beard—scruffy and intentionally unkempt. The last time she saw Anders she suggested he shave it, and he dismissed her. *Mom*, he'd said, his tone jokey. *It's supposed to be sexy.* The word comes back to Ilse now, uncomfortable in a way it hadn't been in her own kitchen. *Sexy*, with its slithering double sibilance and little sigh of a vowel. She turns in her seat so that she is directly facing the young mother, so that the man will see her watching.

"Laissez moi tranquille," the woman says. "S'il vous plait." Of this Ilse understands *me*, and *quiet*, and *please*.

The man only smiles, and when he does, the beard pulls back and a pair of pink lips appears. He lays his fingers on the woman's shoulder, squeezes.

"Casse-toi!" the woman shouts.

A few heads lift, and the man withdraws, puts his hands up—not guilty. He shakes his head at the audience of other riders as if to say, *She's crazy, this one!* Sitting back in his seat, he opens his magazine again as if nothing has happened.

Everyone looks away. The train has not stopped. The child in the woman's lap has not awakened.

Ilse's heart, however, is a racket in her chest. She wants to stand and scream. At her side Joel sits with his eyes closed, his ears stuffed with the noise of his audio tour.

"Are you—" Ilse cranes toward the aisle, toward the woman. "Are you okay?" She fumbles for some French. "Êtes-vous d'accord?"

The woman scowls. "Foutez-moi la paix," she hisses. Her face is flushed. She turns to the window.

Ilse sits back as if she's been slapped. She is light-headed. *Foutez-moi. Foutez-moi.* What does it mean? She grips the seat to stem the spinning.

"What's happening?" Joel asks. He removes his earbuds. "Are you okay?" He coils the earbud cord neatly and tucks it away in his pocket, then gets up to sit beside her, putting his arm around her shoulders.

"Don't touch me," Ilse says.

"Are you motion sick?"

"Oh god." She puts her head between her knees.

"Just breathe through your nose," Joel says, rubbing her back.

"I said don't touch me."

For the rest of the ride he holds on to her though, and when they get out at the station, he keeps his hand on her elbow as they cross the street. The nearest restaurant is, horribly, a McDonald's, and he seats her at a table and brings her a latte and a hot croissant, which he watches her eat, concern on his face.

"You were just over-hungry," he says. "Low blood sugar probably. I shouldn't have rushed you earlier. We should have stopped at that place near the hotel. There would have been time for a bite." He looks truly remorseful, and this softens her.

"I'm fine," Ilse says. "It's nothing. Don't worry about me."

"I do worry. I do."

When they go outside it is raining. They must walk to the palace—not a long walk, but he debates getting a cab and wonders aloud if she can make it. She can hear his disappointment in his voice; he has been excited, and now she's ruining the day.

A cab would be ridiculous, but she agrees to let him buy her an umbrella at a tourist shop, and they set out, him holding the crooked handle between them.

"The palace was a hunting lodge to begin with," Joel says as they walk. "Louis the Thirteenth built it in the seventeenth century. It covers over two thousand acres, total. Over seven hundred thousand square feet of living space, though maybe that's not all actual living space. No one *lived* in the Hall of Mirrors, for instance, though it was used regularly for royal parties and celebrations."

He has memorized the audio tour. *Foutez-moi*, Ilse thinks. *Foutez-moi. Foutez-moi.* Her steps and the rain and Joel's incessant factual monologue all beat in rhythm to these words.

He goes on. "Apparently a massive windstorm took out a significant portion of the landscaping on the property in 1999, but the French citizenry paid to plant something like fifty thousand new trees." His pace quickens as he talks, and Ilse must almost jog to remain beneath the umbrella. "Imagine how that would've gone in America." Joel chuckles.

"I'm not sure what you mean." Ilse stops and the umbrella wobbles ahead of her until Joel realizes she's pausing and steps back. "The *citizenry* pays for things all the time in the US. We have incredible national parks. Haven't you ever been to Yosemite? The Grand Canyon? Otto and I took the children to all the western parks, and they were stunning. Really stunning. We put our money to preservation, not—" She waves a hand in the air before her face. "Not pomp."

Joel frowns. "I thought you wanted to come here."

She sighs. She doesn't even care about this, but it's irritating her now—all of it: his facts and his obvious pleasure in knowing them, the rain and the cold and the reality that she's just drunk a McDonald's coffee in France. And also the train ride. Still the train ride. *Foutez-moi. Foutez-moi.*

"I'm just tired," she says. "Forget it."

He takes her elbow again, but he looks like a child she's just chastised. "We're nearly there," he says.

At the palace they pass through the enormous golden gates, and Joel flashes an attendant the tickets he took time to buy yesterday in town to avoid a line today. There is no line, though—just a Japanese tour group and a pair of old ladies in matching red rain jackets.

He hands Ilse the umbrella and unzips his coat to find his tour brochure. "Our package includes the gardens, the Grand Trianon, and Petite Trianon," he reads. "But it begins with the chateau." He gestures at the central entrance to the palace, where suited employees stand guard at the door.

Ilse hesitates. She imagines Joel's hand on her arm for the next hour, his voice in her ear with more facts. "I think I'll walk the gardens. The rain won't bother me, and I'd really love to see the gardens again," Ilse says. "But you enjoy the tour. I'll find you." Before he can say another word, she slips her ticket from his hand and turns.

"You don't want to see the Hall of Mirrors?" Joel calls from behind her.

She waves, smiles. "Keep your phone on. I'll text you at lunchtime."

Her feet crunch over the gravel as she rounds the path leading to the gardens. Overhead, it is only drizzling now, and so she keeps the umbrella folded. The palace is startlingly pink in this odd winter light. She doesn't remember that from the last visit. What does she remember? It's all vague. A walk down a long dirt road to Marie Antoinette's hamlet. The children stopping to examine ladybugs in the grass, and to play a game of hide-and-seek behind the evenly planted trees along the roadside. She remembers the day as windy. She kept trying to put a summer sun hat on fair little Anders, and by the end of the day the hat was lost, left somewhere in the expanse of the gardens. She remembers Sylvie asking loudly why all the statues of the gods were naked and, later, in the Hall of Mirrors, making faces at herself in the glass. She remembers Anders boosted onto Otto's shoulders, giggling at the two-headed reflection he and his father made, then reaching at the air, enchanted by the movement of the golden light refracting from the mirrors like a live, caged thing.

Ilse has an impulse to call them, her children, and as she walks, she slips her phone from her pocket before remembering that she can't call home so easily. There's the expense, and the time difference. What time is it at home? She tries to calculate, but her thoughts feel sluggish and muddled. *Nine hours*, she remembers Joel saying when they booked their flight. She counts and comes up with evening. She pictures Sylvie feeding her husband and their boys dinner. There's likely still homework to be done, school forms to be signed, lunches to be prepared for tomorrow. It's barely controlled chaos. Sylvie won't be free to really talk for at least another two hours, when the children have been bathed and read to, and by then she won't want to talk. *Oh hi, Mom*, she'll say, her voice distant and distracted. Ilse remembers what it is to reach that time of day and find yourself exhausted, every particle of your energy and thought expended on the care of others.

She next considers Anders, but he won't even be home from work yet, or is sitting in Seattle traffic, the music turned up loud and racketing in his little tuna can of an efficiency car, his phone inaudible. They're both busy with their lives, which is as it should be. It's her success that they do not need her now. She palms the phone and keeps it shut off but still in her hand as she walks, the way she sometimes holds on to a smooth, cold stone when she walks the beach at home.

In the garden the orange trees are noticeably absent, shuttled into the Orangerie for the season. The gravel paths are wide and bare, their symmetry even more evident without the trees. When she last saw them, these gardens were her favorite part of the tour. She was the harried mother of young children, wife of a man who'd married his dreams—his ambition—long before he married her, and her daily life was made up of so much banal disorder, each day a series of expected but uncontrollable routines. From behind the fog of that reality, the gardens had seemed a living liturgy—proof of the possibility that symmetry could be achieved within wildness, and also evidence that beauty might still be wrested from repetition. She had read somewhere once that the gardens were intended to serve as a visual demonstration of the king's dominance over his land and so, more largely, of man's dominance over nature. It was a lofty claim, but she could see the appeal then, when so much of her life felt undetermined, moored to nothing but the unpredictable present and her terrifyingly consuming love for three people, who would all one day (it was the only certainty) leave her.

As she passes now through the measured curves of the garden, she remembers details of that last trip. Anders had caught a cold just before they left home, and so Ilse worried over him through their first week in France, fearing she'd have to call a doctor, deal with a medical system she didn't understand, try to use her meager French to explain her son's allergy to penicillin if it turned out to be strep throat. Sylvie was well but a handful. She ran ahead of Otto at the Louvre and was lost for several minutes in a crowd of tourists. She also had a tantrum of epic proportions in a park near their rented apartment, and in the heat of Ilse's embarrassment and frustration, she spanked Sylvie there within sight of the other parents, who all politely looked away. Later, Sylvie tossed a shoe into the Seine, and Ilse struggled to carry both her and Anders back to the apartment alone, but Otto was on an excursion with his students, unavailable to help with any parenting duties. She recalls the clamp of fury in her chest as she lugged the children—Sylvie in her arms and Anders strapped to her in a toddler backpack—through the crowded streets of their borrowed neighborhood. And, with thin remorse, she remembers the tirade she unleashed on Otto that evening when he returned from his class.

They'd come to Versailles only on the last day of their trip and had afterward gone back to their apartment in the city and packed their bags for home. That night they were awakened by one of Otto's students whose roommate had drunk herself unconscious. Because the student was female and sick, and because of her medical training, Ilse had been the one to go to the dorms to care for her. On the flight home the next morning she was exhausted, impatient with the children's whining and the tedium of travel, her head aching for rest and for silence.

Why has she remembered that trip so fondly, then? For years she and Otto talked about returning. They thought of that summer they'd spent in France as a highlight of their family's life together. They both had—not just Ilse—and so there must have been more to it than tantrums and weariness and those first, dim glimmers of their own brokenness as a couple.

She huffs out a cloud of breath and turns on the phone in her hand, dials. The pushing silence of vacancy registers for a moment before a click, and then his voice.

"Who is this?" Otto says.

"I'm standing in Louis the Thirteenth's gardens."

Otto's laugh comes through the phone. "It's the middle of the night, Ilse."

"No—" She pauses, the hands of a clock in her head spinning, cartoonish. "But it's not even eleven a.m. here." A wave of embarrassed heat rushes her. She's miscalculated the time difference, run the hours ahead rather than back. How could she have been so stupid? "I'm sorry. I'm sorry I woke you. I had nine hours in my head, but it's the other way around." She hears herself stumbling through this explanation. "Go back to bed."

"I'm awake," Otto says. His voice is easy, charmed even, she thinks, by her mistake. *Of course.* How irritating.

Ilse shakes her head at herself. "It's a bad time to call."

"The children told me you were going to Paris," Otto goes on. "Good for you." His voice is big, the encouragement genuine, and in spite of herself, Ilse is glad to have his blessing. Proud that, of the two of them, she is the one who actually managed this return trip. It contradicts some of the disappointments he raised about her when they were divorcing—that she was too dependent, that she did not see a difference between solitude and abandonment.

Here she is now, doing what they'd planned to do, without him.

"It is good for me," she says. "It's very good for me, thank you."

"A birthday present to yourself, I assume?"

She's pleased that he remembers. "I thought I deserved something big."

"Absolutely," Otto says. "You do." A beat of hesitation. "Is winter in Paris just what we thought it'd be?"

"The Louvre wasn't crowded, if that's what you mean. The sky is broody and gray. You'd probably love it."

He laughs again, an agreement and a concession: She still knows him.

Ilse cradles the phone against her shoulder, pulls her gloves from her bag and slips them on. "It's cold," she says. "Honestly, it's very cold here."

"Right. Winter," Otto says.

"Yes. I think it might snow."

There's the sound of distance between them—that heavy, almost imperceptible hum of a continent and an ocean and too many years. She pictures him rising from his bed, his white hair mussed and his pajamas rumpled. An old man. Or at least an older man.

"Did you make this transatlantic call just to give me the weather report, or was there something I could do for you?" Otto says, the play back in his tone.

"You're sure I didn't wake you?"

"Not at all. I was reading and drinking, but not sleeping. You remember."

"Right," she says, because she does remember. She pictures him pacing the rooms of the little house he bought after the divorce just as he used to pace their shared rooms. Restless. His mind unable to shut off in the dark. He always claimed he liked it—the quiet of the house when everyone else was asleep, which could be so complete it was almost a physical presence. He liked the solitude of night.

Ilse envisions him now at his kitchen window, looking at his own reflection, his eyes smaller seeming without his glasses on, his body frailer inside his clothes than it was even five years ago, when he left her. Age appears to have found him suddenly, and it is diminishing him in ways that it has not yet done to her. Some days this knowledge has the pin-sharp prick of victorious spite; other days it sinks in her, a sorrow over which she no longer has any claim.

She releases a breath. "How do you remember our trip here? What stands out to you about it, I mean."

"Paris is the city of love."

"Oh," she scoffs. "Don't give me that bullshit."

"Really. That's what I remember." Otto's smiling. She can hear his grin through the phone. "Don't you remember that first night in the apartment we rented?" He lets out an audible breath, a still-satisfied sigh. "It was like we'd been starved and could finally eat all we wanted."

"Please," Ilse says, though she is smiling now too, blushing beneath her coat and scarf. Joel, she thinks, would never talk to her this way. Not ever. "It's far too cold here for me to remember anything like that," she says. "Everything is frozen and cold."

"Yes, well. It did turn out that way, didn't it?"

She lets this go and continues. "Come on now. I'm serious. What do you remember?"

"I remember the whole trip as good."

"Why though? That's what I want to know. I need something more specific. Do you remember Sylvie chasing the ducks on the lawn by the Grand Canal here at Versailles?"

He laughs. "That's right. She was a terror, wasn't she? They were both fucking terrors that day. We'd made them be quiet on the train. Anders was about to combust."

She grins. "That wasn't because of the train. That was just Anders."

"He liked Marie Antoinette's hamlet. I remember that. There were carp in the pond, and we had bread from lunch in the pack."

Yes! This comes back to Ilse in stark relief against the gray sky: Ander's blond head leaning over the waters of the green pond, a clot of squashed bread in his fist. He throws the bread and the surface breaks suddenly, raucously, into a hundred smacking, open maws. She sees Anders jolt with the ugliness of the surprise—the horror of the riot, the fish throwing their bodies over one another to get to the bread—and then he shrieks with delighted laughter.

"I remember," she says to Otto.

"It was raining when we first got there, and then the sun came out by afternoon."

"No. It didn't rain."

"I have photos. Probably too many photos, but I must have been excited about the light. There's one of you and Sylvie, actually, looking out a window from inside the palace. There are raindrops still on the glass, and the sun is hitting them just so. It's your face and hers in profile, and you're both looking out this glittering window. It's one of my favorite shots of the trip. You with Sylvie. I framed it."

"You have a framed photo of that trip? How did I miss that all these years?"

"It was up in my office for a long time. It's in the bedroom now, next to one of Anders I took on his twelfth birthday—the birthday we celebrated with cupcakes at the beach. He was so suddenly grown up, but in the picture he has blue icing all around his mouth. You remember."

Ilse lets this sink in—her photograph still hanging on the wall in Otto's bedroom.

Otto clears his throat. "Look, I'm happy to reminisce with you, but I guess I don't understand why you want to do it right now, while you're there with—what's his name? Sylvie mentioned you'd be traveling with your boyfriend. That word's such a bugger, isn't it, when you're as old as we are? *Boyfriend*."

Ilse closes her eyes. There it is—the sting. The distance between them rushes through the phone.

"Is he standing right there beside you now? The boyfriend?"

"He's taking the docent's tour."

"Ah. You can't stand those."

"That's why I'm in the garden."

"So, the trip's going that badly. Sorry. If you need to come home, just leave him and come home."

A slosh of gall stirs in her gut at his presumption. "I just wanted to check my memory," she says. "Nothing's gone wrong here. Joel's fine. He's probably waiting on me, in fact."

"From what Sylvie said, he seems the sort who would stand there waiting. He probably has a map in his hand, too."

"I should go, Otto."

"He's an engineer, right? They love maps, engineers."

"I've got to go."

His good-bye is tinged with disappointment, but instead of feeling pleased by this, she is irritated. How irksome of him to be possessive of her now, to remember his affection for her now. How like him to offer exactly what she needs far too late for it to be of any use to her.

She shoves the phone back into her pocket. While she's been talking, a few more tourists have arrived, and a gardener has set up with a box of pruning tools at the end of the hedgerow. She passes him; passes a school group of giggling teenagers in matching blue-plaid uniforms; passes the still form of the Latona Fountain, its water glassy and the empty open mouths of the bronze turtles and alligators wide and gasping at nothing. She considers calling Otto back to insist, *The trip is going well.* But that would only seem like an embarrassed denial of the truth, and so she leaves the phone in her pocket.

The fact is that the trip *is* going well. Nothing terrible has happened. The airline didn't lose any luggage, the hotel didn't forget their reservation, and every restaurant they've tried has been exactly as the guidebooks and websites promised. It has been, without exception, a note-perfect carrying out of the plans they made, other than the details she herself has spoiled—her refusal, for instance, to wait in line at the Eiffel Tower, and the inexplicable fog of disappointment under which she's been wallowing this morning. For years she has known without any doubt that she was the practical, reasonable, unshakeable half of her marriage, and that it was Otto who was prone to swift turns of emotion and flighty impulses. When they were in the worst of their bad days, it was always this at the heart of their fights. How could she be expected to trust him when he had already made so many reckless decisions? When he spent money wildly at times and without asking her? When he did things like forget to turn up for an agreed-upon meeting or one of the kids' school conferences? And, he would argue back, how could he be expected to share his thoughts with her when she was so rigid, so dismissive of his anxieties as neurotic and his interests as esoteric? When she pestered him like a child about his obligations to the family? When, after nearly forty years together, she was still so reluctant to believe he wouldn't abandon her?

But you did abandon me, she thinks now. *You have.* She stalks forward along the garden path, her face warm and her heartbeat heavy, her arms pumping at her sides. She is in her head, not paying attention, when she clips the shoulder of a 20-something man in a puffy down coat walking the opposite way on the path.

"Watch out!" he says, and he jumps out of her way, goggles his eyes at her as she passes.

Under her breath Ilse whispers, *Foutez-moi*! A hiss like the air going hot out of a spinning tire.

"What was that you said to me?" the man asks. His accent is Irish, his tone spiked in offense. He has stopped in the path to look at her.

Ilse stops, too, and turns. She doesn't know what she's said, and so she stays silent, holding the young man's glare until he throws his hands up and walks off.

Shaken, she makes her way to the next fountain and finds a bench and sits. She unwinds her scarf from around her neck, removes her gloves and sets them one on top of the other in her lap. There's a water bottle in her bag, and she drinks several hungry sips, waiting for her pulse to slow, her flush to fade. "Foutez-moi," she says aloud, just to test the words. They sound obscene, even if they aren't. *Foutez-moi. Foutez-me. Fuck me.* Obscene regret. Obscene frustration.

She thinks again of that last night they spent in France three decades ago. It was after midnight when Otto's student started pounding on their apartment door, her knocks erratic, her calls to him through the door frantic. Ilse remembers Otto's confusion and then his panic. She remembers him hurrying out of their bed in only his boxer shorts and running down the stairs to answer the knocks. For several minutes she lay in bed, just listening. She didn't want the children to wake. She didn't want there to be a scene that would upset the landlady, who was asleep in her own apartment on the other side of the wall.

Most of all, however, she didn't want to hear anything that would throw into question her trust for Otto, though she was already questioning it. He had spent much of their trip off somewhere else, with the students. There had been late nights. He was taking them to see the city. That was his job, he reminded her when she expressed dismay. But here was a young woman crying at the door in the middle of the night. What was she to make of that? Why would a girl come crying to Otto, at this hour, on the last night of their trip? Why, if not something horrible—something shattering? Ilse listened to Otto's voice and the girl's, both impassioned, indistinct, and when she could take it no longer, she got up and put on a robe and descended the stairs herself.

In the end it had been nothing, really. Or not what she had feared, anyhow. She walked with the girl back to the dorms, and it took only a few knocks on the other students' doors to learn that the lost roommate had said she was going to a club several hours earlier, that she had indeed come back to the dorms in a taxi just after eleven. The dorm's security guard could confirm that, and he could also get Ilse a spare universal key. He walked with her and the still-teary girl as they opened every door on the second-floor corridor until they found the missing roommate, alive but passed out in a pool of vomit on a vacant bed.

Much of that night is gone now, having dissolved the way unimportant details of even distinct memories do. But she does recall the smell of the room when she opened the door—the high, sweet smell of wine mingled with the overwhelming stench of vomit, of feces. The girl had passed out facedown. Her skirt was pulled up over her hips so that her bare backside was exposed. It was shocking—and also very ordinary. A drunk college student abroad. Nothing unexpected there. But the smell—which was so grossly human, so bodily and messy—and the girl's tanned bottom—which was (Ilse remembers thinking this) so round and young and perfect, but also soiled with her own waste—these were shocking. *We have to wake her up*, Ilse remembers saying, but the male guard would not enter the room, and the roommate, who had been so worried before, could only gag.

Had Ilse hauled the girl out of bed on her own? Had she shaken the girl awake? Those details are gone too. Somehow she got the girl off the bed. Somehow she got her into a bathroom. There's a vision at the back of her mind of the girl sitting fully clothed on the floor of a shower stall, the water running pink around her knees as the red wine she'd vomited into her hair washed away down the drain. *Wake up, honey*, Ilse kept saying, her voice almost a shout against the tiled walls as she waited for the cold water to work. *You need to wake up.* And eventually the girl opened her eyes, and Ilse got her clothes over her head and some shampoo worked into her hair, and then the two of them walked back to the dorm room, where the girl waited as Ilse cleaned up the bed and remade it for her. *Just go*, the girl said, once it was all over. She looked at Ilse with contempt, not gratitude. *Just go and leave me alone.*

Something like that. She had said something like that, and Ilse had felt slapped, stunned at the girl's ingratitude and at her own apparent invisibility.

By the time she left the girl, it was nearly dawn, the sky just washing blue and rosy gold over the old buildings of Paris, and on the way back to Otto and the children, she stopped at a café just opening its doors. She sat at a sidewalk table and ordered a coffee and pretended for a few moments that she had not just spent the night cleaning up a stranger's sick, that she was not about to spend a full day aboard a plane with two small children, but that this was her life instead—early morning walks and breakfast alone.

She is still sitting on the bench in the garden, remembering that coffee and chain of thoughts, when Joel appears, his tour finished, a worried look on his face. "How're you feeling?" he asks.

"Weary," she says. "But fine. I'm fine."

He sits beside her, lays his hand on her knee.

When they get home, she knows, they won't see each other again. She isn't angry with him. She's not even really bothered by him anymore. But there's nothing ahead for them either. That much has become clear on this trip.

She touches his hand. "I love this fountain," she says. "I've always thought it the best of the bunch. The collection."

"It's Apollo on his chariot. Louis the Fourteenth had it built on an existing pond. Apollo is the god of the sun, so this fountain faces east-west. And Louis was known as the sun king."

Ilse lets him go on, the facts forming, floating, and dissolving around her, fragile and inconsequential and not of her concern.

She has not been really looking at it, but now she turns her eyes to the fountain in front of her. The water is a serene sheet of silver light, and rising from it—as if they've been drowned down below for ages—are the straining bodies of four big horses, the triumphant god ascendant in the air. Ilse can feel their thunder in her chest, just as she did when she first saw this fountain, and it's as startling as ever, this stilled motion, this still unresolved contradiction.

Eclipse

This is how I first saw her: I was standing on the shore. It was an early spring morning, but gray. This was not long after the light disappeared for good. The sky was the color of my grandmother's pewter pitcher, or the inside of an oyster's dirty shell. Where heaven met earth, some alders made a rickrack of black lace, and fog topped the water like the layer of fluff inside a new bottle of pills.

Imogen was the first to step out of the waves—bathing cap first, then white neck and arms. When she took off the cap, her pale braid fell down her back. She had the high step of a seabird picking its way across the sand.

It took a minute for the other girls to separate themselves from her, one after the other slipping out of Imogen's body, like a deck of cards splaying in a fan, or a paper chain unfolding. One, two, three, four—they kept falling from her, until soon they were all visible, the whole company of eight girls, identical and standing in a line on the rocky stripe of beach.

Other than my mother's, they were the first ghosts I'd ever seen.

Unlike Imogen, I live on land. My house is four rooms and a porch. It has wood floors and a fireplace, a kitchen that smells like onions, a bay bush growing by the back door. It's at the end of a dirt road on the western side of an island on the western side of a continent.

My house is not really my house. It belongs to my grandmother, who is not my grandmother but is the woman my mother called "mother." She is small and wide set and strong. She can cut a cord of firewood in one day's work. She can sew a dress just my size, measuring only with her eyes. She can bake a loaf of bread that tastes like heaven. She is faithful to me and to God above all else. My grandmother wears her still-dark hair in a chin-length blunt cut, the same as I wear mine, because she's the one who takes the scissors to both our heads. She likes to say, "Blood isn't what matters," and this is what I told Imogen that first day on the beach when she asked why I wasn't afraid of her. "Blood isn't what matters."

Imogen lifted her slim hand and struck it hard against the black barnacles that crust the beach rocks. Her skin split—a little fissure—but only a fine strand of white grains poured from the cut. "I'm made of salt," she said.

I shrugged and offered her the hem of my skirt to wipe her palm against, but she put the gash to her lips and sucked.

"Like Lot's wife," I said. She didn't know the story, and so I told her: "There was a woman who had to leave her home. God told her, 'Don't look back,' but the woman couldn't help herself. When she looked over her shoulder and saw her town burned to ash, she was transformed into a pillar of salt." I nodded at Imogen. "Now you tell me something."

Imogen frowned. Even then, when we were new to each other, I could read her thoughts as if they were printed out in neat script. I could see all of her and—through her—all of everything else.

"Once," she began, "there were two girls—sisters—born at the same time."

"Twins, then," I said.

"Of a sort. One sister was born of a mother in the usual way. The midwife lay the infant in a crib near a window, and as soon as the sunlight fell through that window and onto the first baby, the second baby was born, her sister, a shadow."

"And?" I asked.

"And what?" Imogen said. "That's the story."

"Nothing's happened yet."

She smiled, shrugged her cloudy shoulders. "It's what I can tell you now."

This was unsatisfying, and for a moment I was irked at her for hoarding the story.

"Let's skip rocks," she said, though, and as if she'd been hoarding them, too, she handed me a palm full of perfect skipping stones, each of them gray and wound round with one white band.

At the edge of the water, where the foam piles up white-brown like a lip of bubbled milk, we stood shoulder to shoulder and threw in our stones. They broke the skin of the water and sent out even ripples, one circle erupting from the next, before the hole sealed over again, slick and still, steel gray as our sky.

There are too many ideas about our darkness to name them all.

"For at one time you were darkness, but now you are light," I have heard the pastor read at church. And also, from Matthew, "The sun will be darkened, and the moon will not give its light; the stars will fall from the sky, and the heavenly bodies will be shaken."

Meanwhile, the scientists talk about an obstructive body. "Imagine a lake of dust," they say, "floating in orbit between the Earth and the sun."

Perhaps it's ash, some think—the result of a volcanic eruption on a distant planet.

More believe we've done this to ourselves, our waste a cloud veil that covers the sun's face during the day, and at night obscures the moon and stars.

I don't yet know what I believe.

Soon, my grandmother tells me, if the light doesn't return, the grass and the flowers will stop growing. The trees will stop putting out leaves. The wire bramble of blackberries that fence the road leading to our place will stop fruiting, and the animals will disappear. I know this, but it frightens me to hear her say it.

Already, the tourists have stopped taking the ferry to our island. No one wants to pay to see a beach in the dusk. No one wants to stand on the corner by Queenie's Market and eat ice cream in the chill of the afternoon's darkness. The summer houses along the beach road have all been shut up, and the stores are closing, too, one by one, because there's just not enough business to keep the doors open. Even longtime island people have left—the man who delivered our mail for years, Ms. Vorlean from the bookstore, my teacher. There are empty houses on every street, and the people who haven't left mostly stay inside now. Fear grows where there's no information, my grandmother says, but it doesn't make sense to me why the school had to close, why the library shut its doors. The only place you can still go is church, which I suppose some people find comforting.

"We'll be fine," my grandmother says to reassure me. "We have our faith and we're resourceful, you and I. We'll manage."

I wonder, though. Our backyard garden did poorly this year. The potatoes were the size of walnuts, the carrots small and pale. And the rabbits and deer completely devoured anything above ground, they were so hungry. My grandmother has a pantry full of canned goods still, but I know we'll eat through them quickly once the rest is gone.

"It won't be forever until the light returns," my grandmother says again and again. "Everything has its season, and every season ends." She kisses me on the head just as she kissed my mother the night she disappeared. One kiss on the crown of my head.

Sometimes I feel the strength of the kiss run down the center of my body like a stake going right through me, a peg rooting me to this place.

Other times I think she's a dowser and the kiss is a rod, testing me: *Is there anything of value left here in this body?* the kiss asks. *Has this girl gone empty yet?*

Not yet.

Imogen soon became my only friend. Sometimes I passed the houses of my old friends on my way to the beach. Behind their closed curtains, the blue-green lights of televisions flashed. They wanted to stay in the old world, I realized. One where the difference between day and evening was more than a change of grays. They wanted glare and squint. Heat on the cheeks and shoulders. Sunglasses and burns. The sparkle of a reflection playing off someone's wristwatch, or the square of afternoon light unfolding on the floor beneath the window. I knew because I wanted that, too, but for me watching it flattened on a TV screen would never be enough.

The other truth is that those children hadn't ever really been my friends. Their mothers knew about my mother well before I did, and they didn't want her influence in their homes. That's the way my grandmother said it to me: "They don't want her influence in their homes," as if, like my shadow, my mother trailed behind me always. No one had ever been cruel, but they avoided me, and so I became used to being alone.

Maybe this is why Imogen seemed so wonderful to me. I wanted to be with her, in her presence, all the time. As soon as my grandmother freed me from breakfast to run outside, I went to the beach. I couldn't call to her—the water between us would only swallow my voice—and so I took to standing on the sand, still as a heron, watching the water for signs of her. When she did finally spot me, she'd emerge from the sea like a person climbing up a staircase from a basement, head, shoulders, torso, legs. Behind her, her sisters always followed.

One afternoon a few days after we met, I asked, "What does it look like below the water? Is it just darkness there too?"

We were sitting side by side on a tumble of bleached driftwood. The sand flies jumped like fleas at my feet, more sluggish in the cooler temperature than they used to be. I shooed them away. Behind us, Imogen's sisters had arrayed themselves along another log, one girl in front of the next, all of them focused on grooming one another. I watched them finger-combing tiny shrimp and bits of seaweed from one another's hair. Next, they'd set to work on their elaborate braids. This was their routine.

"Is it dark at your house too?" I asked again.

"I don't know how to answer that," she said. "Yes and no."

She told me about the plankton that glittered like stars. At night, she said, when even the little light from my sky overhead disappeared and the surface of the water went true black and endless, only then was it possible to see them—tiny animals, each an ember. They moved in currents, she said, like ribbons of light threading the waves. Like the veined band of the Milky Way. I pictured it. We'd lost our moon just like our sun. We'd lost all our constellations.

"Bioluminescence," I told her. "It's a chemical reaction." I explained what I had learned in sixth-grade science class, before the light left, when I was still going to school. I was good at science, and I loved it. Wasn't science, after all, just asking questions? We learned about motion and energy, the solar system and the atom. We made simple machines from paper tubes and rubber bands and coat hangers. We built atomic models, egg-suspension inventions, and balsa-wood boats that we sailed in a plastic baby pool in our classroom. I remembered it all now the way I remembered so many of the details from life before the light left—like my mind had all along been a storage room in which I was hiding things away. I'd forgotten what was in there until the darkness outside forced me to turn on the lamp and look around.

I told Imogen what I knew about bioluminescence—about fireflies and lantern fish and siphonophores, which look like single jellyfish but are actually colonies of many organisms. "They use the light they make to camouflage themselves, or to speak to other animals. It's a code they can signal with their bodies."

"Colonies?" she asked. She tipped her head the way a listening animal might do, frowned. The feathered gosling-gray down of her eyebrows furrowed.

"Communities. Groups. Many rather than one."

"I know the word," she said. "I meant why."

I repeated my teacher's words: "They work together to keep the whole body alive."

"Like my sisters and me," Imogen said. The girls all turned their faces to her at the mention. "I require them, and they require me."

"I don't understand."

"I require my sisters. All of them." She looked at me with her pale eyes and took my hand in hers. I could see our skins touching, but I felt nothing.

I thought of how, when I was a little girl, I liked to climb into my mother's bed in the morning. She had the bed that is now mine and kept it in the room that is now mine too—the east-facing bedroom. When it was out, the sun always fell first through her bedroom window, and lying beside my sleeping mother, I liked to pass my fingers into and out of the square of light the window cast on the quilt. Light/dark. Warm/cool. My mother's hand/my own. The light was both nothing and not-nothing on my skin, just like Imogen's grasp.

"Are you here or not here?" I asked her.

"Here."

"And when you go back into the water?"

She smiled. "Is the sun gone just because you can't see it?" She pointed up and I followed her finger. The sky was thick, the color of wet sand, a cave wall. I couldn't be sure what lay beyond it.

"I don't know," I said. Again, I thought of my mother. She left in the middle of the night. The last time I saw her, she hit my grandmother—struck her across the face. She'd wanted money, and my grandmother said no. The pills my mother took had made her sick and thin and pale, a parallel and sometimes violent ghost of herself. "I don't know," I repeated.

Imogen's fingers laced between my own. "You know more than you think you do."

Later, once Imogen's sisters had folded back into her like a string of paper dolls stacking and she/they slipped back into the waves, I walked home in the dark, moving my arms in front of me as if I were swimming too, my fingers combing the cool air, pushing me forward, forward, forward through the trembling cone of my headlamp's single beam.

It was early summer when the ferry stopped making its run between our island and the mainland each day. We'd been without sun for six months by then, and without sun we were without tourists, and without tourists there wasn't enough revenue to pay for the fuel. The state's department of transportation suspended all ferry operations. A few more island families gave up, packed their belongings in crates, and got on the last boat leaving. Several of us went to the dock to see them off.

My grandmother's friend Lena was one of the departures. She had a son on the mainland, and he'd offered to make room for her in his house. At the boat that morning, seeing Lena off, my grandmother looked puffy-faced and weary. She and Lena had known each other since they were girls. "She's making a mistake," my grandmother said as she waved to Lena, who had climbed aboard the boat, disappeared, and reappeared a few moments later on the upper deck. "She'll see. It will be worse over on the other side."

"You think so?" I asked. I wasn't thinking of Lena so much as my mother. We didn't know where she'd gone when she left, but it was somewhere on the other side.

"Oh, yes. Yes, I do." My grandmother had put a cotton scarf around her neck as we'd left our house, and its blue and yellow flowers seemed shockingly bright against the gray sky, white boat, brown wooden dock railings. I was still getting used to seeing in sepia. I wasn't sure I ever would.

"Why do you say that?" I asked. "What have you heard?" But my voice was drowned out by the blow of the ferry's low, keening horn and the sudden thunder of its massive engines churning to a start. I leaned over the dock railing and watched the water roil, a skirt of frothing white bubbles and rolling waves ruffling outward from the ferry's hull. I thought of Imogen and her sisters there under the water, the massive body of the boat like a shadow, but white. It reminded me of how, in the days when the sun rose and hung at the apex of the sky, passing clouds cast shadows onto the fields. These shadows moved like barges over the tall grass on a summer day, real and not real at once. Maybe that's what boat bottoms looked like to Imogen and her sisters. Maybe our whole world was little more than shadow to them, the way they were to me. On the dock, I put my clammy fingertips to my arm to check for my own materiality, but there I was—skin and bone and fine blond hairs—just as always.

"You okay?" my grandmother asked me.

I nodded, and she took my hand, and we walked home together.

That night, I couldn't sleep. Before I closed my eyes, I thought of my mother—not as a woman, but as a little girl. Wild eyes and stringy hair and dirty feet. Girl abandoned and alone, found in an empty house on the south side of the island, screaming like a feral cat. My grandmother had claimed her body and kept that safe, but you can't claim someone else's fear. That had stayed with my mother always. I fell asleep thinking, *You can't claim someone else's fear*, and so I dreamed fear. In one dream I was on a boat made of paper and rowing for my life, but before I could reach the shore of the mainland, the water dissolved my boat's bottom, cold water rushing up around my ankles. I woke with a gasp, certain that my feet were wet. When I finally fell back asleep, I dreamed of another boat, only this time it wasn't me on board but my mother, looking as she had before the sickness took her, her face still full and beautiful, her long hair and yellow dress blowing behind her with the sea breeze. I called to her from the beach, but she had no oars, and the tide was pulling back from the lip of the shore, her boat drawing farther and farther away from me until soon she was just a bright, golden spot out on the horizon. This last dream was vivid, and I couldn't shake the film of unease it left behind in me, and so I got up and went to the kitchen for a piece of bread to settle my stomach.

My grandmother was sitting at the table. Only her hands and the embroidery hoop she was holding were lit in the orange circle of the lamp's light. "What are you doing up?" she asked.

At the counter I cut myself a thick slice of the bread she'd made that morning and buttered it. I thought: *There won't be butter much longer.* I was angry with myself for thinking it. Why did every thought have to be trailed by its negative now?

"I can't sleep," I said.

She made a grumble of sympathy. "Sit with me."

I pulled my chair out from the table and watched her sew as I ate. Her fingers whipped tiny knots into the white fabric. A picture of a forest was rising on the surface of the cloth. Evergreen and lime and goldenrod and blue. Trees and wildflowers and the spotted outline of a stream coming into being, one knot at a time.

"Do you think we should have left too?" I asked.

"No," my grandmother said without hesitating or lifting her head. "We live here."

What I wanted to say but couldn't swelled like weather inside my chest. I opened my mouth and took a breath to speak, changed my mind.

"You don't have to tell me," my grandmother said. "I know what you're thinking. You imagine I don't miss your mother? Worry about her? And now Lena too." She clicked her tongue, sound of disapproval and disappointment—at their choices or our circumstances, I wasn't sure.

"No," I said. Fury flamed to life in my gut. I felt myself turn torch, turn conflagration. My face would light the house. I touched my cheeks, took a breath. "No," I said again. "Why should we worry about the people who chose to leave? I'm only worried about us."

My grandmother set her embroidery in her lap and we sat together in silence for a long time.

"Look at the birds of the air," she said. "They do not sow or reap or store food in barns, and yet they are fed." It was what she'd said to me when my mother left. I remembered.

"Go back to bed now," she said. "One of us, at least, ought to get some rest."

I put my plate on the counter and went to the room that is my room but was my mother's. I lay in the bed and looked up at the ceiling, which was flat and blank and as airless as my body felt. Ash. Char. Salt. "Good night," I called to my grandmother, not because we were usually so formal, but because I needed the sound of her voice returning to me.

"Good night, my love," she called back.

The next day I woke groggy, bleary-eyed, and in a bad mood. I wanted to go immediately to the beach and to Imogen, but it was Sunday, and my grandmother was up and dressed and waiting for me when I stepped out of my room. "I let you have a lie-in," she said. "Service starts in half an hour, though, so get moving."

On our way to church, we saw that a metal chain had been strung across the entrance to the ferry dock, and boards had been nailed over the windows of the ticket office.

"Well, we're stuck now," my grandmother joked. She was wearing her black dress—the one she wore to church every Sunday. Its fabric was dusted with white stars, and its skirt billowed and whirled like clouds of smoke around her shins as we walked. Overnight, her sorrow seemed to have hardened into a resolve about our own survival. "We have enough flour and corn and canned goods put up to last us through next winter, even if they do close the grocery," she said. "We'll be fine."

Speaking certain thoughts aloud also speaks their inversion. In saying, "We'll be fine," my grandmother cast the words *We won't be fine* like a net around us.

At the church there was only a handful of people seated in the pews. Pastor Geraldine shook our hands at the door. "I'm glad to see you're still here, Willie," she said to my grandmother.

"Where else would I be?" my grandmother asked, and the pastor smiled.

The service was short but felt long. The pianist had gone off-island in April, and so we'd been singing the hymns a cappella. Our voices dragged and tugged at one another, out of time and out of tune. In my head I pictured the Portuguese men-of-war that now and then washed up on our beaches—each one actually a colony, and all of them together a stranded flotilla of blue sails on the sand. I pictured the corals of Australia, and the writhing stream of millions of sugar ants I'd once seen climbing the side of a house. I thought of flights of bees and swallows. Hives of cities full of people, all bumbling through the daytime darkness in confusion. *Require* was the word Imogen had used. "I require them," she'd said of her sisters.

In English class, before the darkness, we'd learned about collective nouns, the way they name a community. The water was part of Imogen's community, just as her sisters were. And the piano and the ferry and the sunlight and my mother had all been part of mine. What happened when a colony divided, split? What happened when, like voices dropping from the scale of the chorus one by one, the members of the community vanished? What would become of one without the many?

From the pulpit Pastor Geraldine read the scripture. It was the story of Noah from the book of Genesis. "And every living thing that moved on land perished—birds, livestock, wild beasts, all the creatures that swarm over the earth, and all mankind. Everything on dry land that had the breath of life in its nostrils died. Every living thing on the face of the earth was wiped out." All but Noah, Pastor Geraldine told us. She described a drowned Earth.

Trees and mud and houses swept up by the floodwater. Sky and sea reunited and as endless as they'd been before God swept a hand over the world and divided them, dark from light, dirt from stream, chaos into order.

I closed my eyes and pictured it. Light from the sky falling on the water, a salting of jewels. I saw Noah's boat cutting through the waves and leaving behind only its blazing wake.

"As long as the earth endures, seedtime and harvest, cold and heat, summer and winter, day and night, will never cease," she read. She looked out at those of us gathered and nodded.

It's a lie, I wanted to say. *It's all ending. It's all ended.* But from somewhere in the front pew, a voice sang out the first note of the closing hymn. When it had finished, my grandmother touched my shoulder. The cluster of us who had gathered then stood and shuffled out into the dim late morning.

After the service I convinced my grandmother to let me skip lunch. I wasn't hungry. I couldn't have eaten if I'd wanted to. Some Sundays I felt the words of the scripture pour like cool water over my head. On those days I could walk out of church with peace still fresh on my face like dew on the grass in the morning, and all day I could feel its slow evaporation off my skin. But today I was still ablaze, nothing settled in my head or my gut.

What I needed to understand was where the light had gone. When Noah's flood washed over the earth, the land had not stopped existing. It was there, under the water, waiting for God to invert the storm and draw back the curtain of sea. Where was the light now, then? In my science class, we had learned that light is energy traveling from the sun, and that in a closed system like the Earth's, energy cannot be created or destroyed but can only change form.

I considered this as I walked to the beach. If our light had been covered, like a candle beneath a basket, it was still there, on the other side of whatever was separating us. If it had been converted, transformed like water into ice or steam, its new body could be found and returned to us.

The only true end would be a betrayal, a theft—God cutting a hole in the heavens and reaching through to disappear the sun in his fist. God the destroyer.

I didn't want that God.

I ran to the beach. I felt the heat in my face and thought: Energy. If I could keep running—run all the way around the island again and again and again—could I light myself up? I imagined my face like a lantern, incandescent, illuminated and illuminating. "May God's face shine on you and be gracious to you" were the words of the benediction Pastor Geraldine used each week to send the congregants out into the world. As if the sun were God's face, now turned away from us, and from the misery we felt at this absence.

"Imogen!" I yelled when I reached the shoreline. "Imogen! I need you!"

But this time, she didn't emerge from the water. It was thick and placid. Here and there, where a blade of kelp or a bit of washed-out driftwood bobbed, a pin-tuck dimpled its matte surface, but it remained otherwise undisturbed, the beach empty but for me.

I could wait, I thought, or I could go to her this time.

I pulled the knots of my shoelaces, peeled my socks from my feet like damp fish skins come away from the flesh. My dress, which was too small for me now, I had to wrestle from my body, and once I was free of it, I flung it down in a blue heap on the rocks. I stood in my underwear, my tank, nothing between me and the water but a few feet of sand.

I had swum in this sea many times. My mother had always told me I'd been born in it, though I wasn't sure I believed her. "I felt you were coming," she'd said, "and so I walked down to the beach and stood in the water. It was August. It was so hot. The cold and the waves took the pain away. I needed to take the pain away." These things she whispered into my ear those mornings when we lay together in her bed, now my bed. The sun was warm on those mornings, pouring into the room through the window the way water pours from a faucet. I felt it fill the spaces between our limbs as well. It glazed my mother's face in honeyed light, her freckles pink-orange spots on her cheeks and nose and forehead and chin, her hair the color of strawberry milk spread out on the pillow. My mother's skin always smelled like sweat and ginger, tasted like salt.

Now, at my back, the wind nudged me out of my memory, pushing me forward down the beach. I stepped around the barnacled rocks. Under my weight water welled up, fanning out in dark stars on the sand. A rill of goose bumps lifted along my spine, my arms.

"Imogen!" I called again. The water licked at my toes, my ankles. I pushed my feet forward until they disappeared. The brown-white foam locked around my shins. My knees tingled with the needles of cold. I thought of the ice fur I'd seen form on the windows of our house in midwinter. I kept walking out. The fabric of my underwear soaked through and clung to my skin. My stomach clenched tight against the cold. Now I was in as far as my ribs, my heart. I lifted my feet from the bottom and let the motion of the waves drift me out. "Imogen!" I called.

Here's what else I remembered:

My mother left before the light did. It was summer, so there were hours and hours of extra light; in fact, the days were long and the sun only thickening—pinking like the inner flesh of a melon—as it sank over the edge of the island and melted into the sea.

I knew nothing of my mother's life outside our house, except that she lived more and more of it there—wherever *there* was—and less and less with us. I'd go to sleep alone in the bed we shared but wake in the middle of the night to find her returned to me, sleeping curled against me, her skin sweating a spicy smell, her breath sweet like rotten fruit. She slept in her clothes or in nothing at all. When she was naked, I could see the puckered skin of her belly. I'd left her that way when I'd escaped her, she told me once. I'd left her ugly like that. But I didn't find her belly ugly. The skin there was pale and soft and wrinkled. It gathered around her navel the way fabric gathers when snagged, as if in letting me out of her, she'd had to unravel something of herself. I liked to lie next to my mother when she was sleeping. She was not dangerous asleep. She slept the heavy sleep of an animal, sighing now and then but never waking—not even if I touched my hand to her belly, where I'd once lived. Not even if I put my ear to her chest to listen to the sound of her breathing, as if my mother's body was the shell and she was the secret ocean deep inside it.

That last night, she did not come home for dinner, did not come home to tuck me in. It was my grandmother who combed and braided my hair after my bath, who read to me, who put me into bed and kissed my forehead good night. "Good night," I said, but when she left I got to my knees and parted the curtains and watched the road, waiting for my mother to appear.

I don't know how long I waited, but at some point I fell asleep. When I woke again, it was dark. The sun had gone down and my mother had finally come home. It was her voice that woke me. Her voice like an ax blade on the other side of the bedroom door, bright and hard and angry. Screaming. "Shame," she said. "Wickedness," she said. "Bitch." Words with silver teeth.

I sat up, swung my legs over the side of the bed. Welt of light swelling around the bedroom door. Sound of a dish breaking. Sound of a woman crying, though I didn't know which one—my mother or my grandmother.

"Grandma?" I said.

It was my mother who had thrown the dish. She stood across the room, her back against the wall. She was wet and dripping dark splots of water onto the rug. Her hair clung to her head. In her face her eyes were caverns. Her mouth a dark red hole. And through her thin T-shirt, her nipples were inky stars.

"Go back to bed," my grandmother said.

"Don't you tell her what to do," my mother said. "Don't you tell her. You're not her mother. You're no one's goddamn mother."

Like a comet, she was across the room. She hit my grandmother. One swing.

I don't know if I remember this next piece or if I've invented it, but my mother looks at me. She looks at me, and she is and is not my mother. She is changed. She is standing in front of me, her hand still in the air with the motion of the strike, and she is also at the same time already gone. She is also at the door. She is walking away. Which is the real mother and which is the ghost? I can't be sure. She has split, though, divided. She has peeled one layer of self from the other, and the one still looking at me is dissolving like salt in water, and the one walking out the door is a shade of grainy dust.

"If you go," my grandmother said, "you don't come back."

And that was the end of it. She turned away and went.

My grandmother touched her fingers to her face where my mother had struck her. Split skin beneath her left eye. Smear of blood.

"You're hurt," I said.

"Doesn't matter. I'll be fine. We're both fine."

Inside me, my lungs constricted. The farther out I swam, the harder I had to work to pull in a breath. Water lapped at my neck, at my earlobes. When it entered my ears, my head exploded in white light, and I stopped moving—I must have stopped moving.

Under the water, it was like night. My eyes burned with the salt. Gray and green and brown. Flecks of plant matter and sand stirred up by the motion of the waves and long strands of slim sea grass like hair.

Imogen?

But she didn't appear.

Imogen?

I was too cold to swim, but I lifted my face and held my eyes open against the sting.

Bright blue sparkler trails. Fists of glitter tossed into the waves. Iridescent veins.

My head throbbed with the cold, and my throat—my throat ached.

Imogen?

My grandmother's voice fell like a whisper through the batting of the water.

I reached up my hand and broke the surface.

What I know now is that there is always going to be the time before. I used to be afraid of it following me. I felt it like an animal whose leash I could not let go of, like crows roosting in the trees just over my shoulders.

"We are made of the same dust," my grandmother has said. *We* meaning all of us, but—I always added silently to myself—particularly those who share our blood. At one point I was part of my mother's own body. A stitch in her side, and then a swelling in her middle. It was only her body that kept me safe. I was heart and lungs and brain and bone kept on this side of death only by the thinnest barrier of my mother's own body. And that's not much, when you really think about it—muscle and skin and bone and blood. It returns to dust just as easily as it manifests from it.

When I finally told this to my grandmother, the night I almost drowned, she bent down and kissed my forehead. I was on her lap, like a little girl again. "It isn't blood that matters," she said.

She had carried me home from the beach on her back, stripped me of my wet clothes, and wrapped me in a blanket the color of flame. Now she held me, warming me with her own heat.

"No," I agreed. "I know that. It isn't blood that matters."

I thought of Imogen and her sisters. They required one another, and I required them—until I didn't. What had happened to me in the moment the cold had rushed in? Floating there, under the water, I had thought: *I am nothing but a shadow.* I saw myself dissolving. I would disintegrate. I would be the particulate in the water's current. I would trail the bellies of passing boats, a wake of saline lace. I had closed my eyes, ready. But then, stars.

Overhead, as I hadn't seen them since the darkness began, trails of blue glitter. Where the water snagged and pleated and unfurled itself again on the surface, constellations assembled and dispersed, realigned elsewhere. The world had flipped, swallowed me or lifted me, or both. I let out the last of the breath I'd been holding and watched the bubbles, each outlined in blue light, rise. I stretched out my arms and followed them up to where my grandmother was reaching for me.

"I saw the bioluminescence," I told my grandmother.

"Isn't it beautiful?" she asked.

"You've seen it?"

"Of course. I've lived here all my life."

"I thought it was the sky. Just for a minute."

She shrugged. "One thing isn't that different from another."

"It made me happy again, until I hit the surface and realized."

"There's nothing wrong with being happy," my grandmother said. She kissed my forehead again and pulled the orange blanket closer around me. It was a comfort to be held.

I thought: *There's always going to be the time before, but there is also now.*

Outside our windows the gray of late afternoon was thickening to the silt-dark of dusk. Not a star was visible. Not yet.

Wind Phone

Report: *Wasting Syndrome (SSWS) in Pisaster Ochraceus*
Location: *Dog Island Research Station, Puget Sound, 48.5607° N, 122.7623° W*

Author: *Liis Reishus, PhD, Affiliated Researcher, Dept. of Marine Ecology, University of Washington.*

People like to believe they have influence over disasters, catastrophes, losses—by which they mean control—but that's illusion, and she was done with illusion. Could she write that in her report? *You're all suffering under an illusion.* Instead, she picked up the phone and texted: *Island//illusion. Illusion//island. They sound the same when you say them enough. There's a word for that, but I can't remember it now. I can't remember anything clearly. All my words are inverted and mirrored.*

edrorrim. See? Take your picture with your phone, and you reverse yourself. Is it still you? Send. The words rose on the phone's screen like detritus bobbing to the surface of the sea and floated, unanswered.

In the hours after dark, her last night on the island, she lay on the floor of the research station's sleeping quarters with her phone positioned over her heart, her arms and legs spread wide, her body made star. *Asteroidea-sapien*, she named herself. She gave herself license to name everything, like a colonist. Like a mother. She needed to pin it down to keep it close. This wasn't Dog Island, but Satan's Head. (*Look at the map*, she'd say to anyone who questioned her. *The place has horns.*) The research station: Chambre d'Isolement. The yellow flowers that studded the field beyond the front door: Sneeze-Weed. The stars, the clouds, the wind that was a writhing animal out here at the edge of the sea—all labeled. Each sea star got a name. So did her own body. So did the child—the one that was gone. She said that name aloud like a spell she was casting around herself, protective and possessive: Alena. Daughter.

Again, she picked up the phone and typed: *Did you know that some species of sea stars have the ability to regenerate an amputated arm? Did you know that some stars have the ability to split themselves for reproduction, breaking arm from arm to become one, two, three wholly new individuals?*

From one star, many. Go forth and multiply. I contain multitudes. Blah blah blah. Send. The words materialized in their little amniotic sac on the screen.

On the floor, arms and legs flared to four long points, she said to the rafters, "I'm making myself a star." The crown of her head was just the stub of her missing fifth limb. The missing limb had not killed her, but it would never regenerate.

What she would write in the report was that the imminent reality of dissolution was perhaps proof of health. Who dies but the living, anyway?

Into the phone her fingers typed: *I miss you. What am I going to do?* The words rose and hung in jade suspension on the screen.

But, of course, there was no answer.

The sea stars began disappearing in early 2013. The first reports of a decline in their population came from the Olympic Peninsula of Washington State, then from north in British Columbia, Canada. Fishermen and naturalists who kept informal observation logs started posting alarming counts online. Where there had been hundreds of thousands of stars the year before, there were tens of thousands, then merely thousands, then hundreds, and all of them wasting. Densovirus, the amateurs speculated. There'd been similar plagues in the '70s, on the East Coast and in California, though never as devastating as this one seemed to be. By midspring stars were reported wasting in Oregon, California, Mexico. The virus—if that's what it was—had swept nearly the full North American Pacific coastline in a single season, radically reducing the sea star population. *Why?*

A team of researchers—including faculty from three different university marine biology departments, a NOAA scientist, and a zoologist from an aquarium in Seattle—set out to answer the question. They began taking samples at several coastal posts in BC: populated Victoria and Nanaimo, remote Quadra Island, the Johnstone Strait, the Duke of Edinburgh Ecological Reserve, and the Pacific Rim National Park Reserve. The work was slow going, fastidious. They collected water in plastic tubes and shoveled wasting stars into bags. They mapped out sites between tidepools on the coastal shoreline and counted stars, recording their numbers, planning to return in a week to count again. The disease presented first as lesions, then a whitening of the stars' saturated reds and purples. A diseased arm looked to be netted in a white doily. From there, the creature had hours before its organs began to slide from the inside out. The white goo the disease made of the stars' once bright and rigid bodies, slick as mucus, the researchers collected for examination. They measured water temperature and depth, read tide records for anomalies, compared their data to archives. They tested mollusks and seaweed and sand. The disease only affected the stars, but it affected every species of them in every place sea stars existed. Wasting stars clung, sickly, to the creosote pilings of ferry docks, went slack and sticky between the barnacle-scabbed rocks of pristine preserves, melted like colored lumps of warm candy into the sand at the lip of a beach crowded with screaming children and their umbrella-toting parents. The environmental particulars of the place seemed not to predict the presence of the disease; it was, simply, everywhere.

In April someone in an online forum suggested Fukushima. Hadn't rubble from the Tōhoku earthquake been turning up for the last two years all along the Pacific coast? Car fenders bent like driftwood, traffic signs with Japanese lettering, an entire Harley Davidson motorcycle, children's plastic toys, buoys and glass fishing net baubles and soccer balls. A rusted ship, floating upright and ghostly, uncaptained, through the dawn fog off the coast of BC. Didn't all of that suggest something essential about the westward drift of the current from Asia, and—perhaps—about the possibility of seaborne radioactive residue from the Fukushima meltdown? Maybe it wasn't Densovirus at all? Or maybe not just the virus? Maybe the sweep of the virus had been farther, faster because the toxicity of the water had damaged the stars' immune responses?

A journalist picked this up, then concerned citizens carried it like hysteria through the traffic of internet forums. For a month there was a panic. Everyone along the entire coastline had been in the water—fishermen and researchers and children and marine enthusiasts. Was the water toxic? News sites ran stories that posed the question. Coastal villages shuttered their beaches until further notice.

This wasn't it, though, it turned out. The water tested negative. It was something else.

Time passed without any progress.

Then, it was late spring, a year after the first wasting stars were documented—June of 2014. By this time the stars had nearly vanished up and down the Pacific coastline of North America. They had vanished everywhere but one just-discovered location: Dog Island. Researchers went out to investigate. Dog Island was a sanctuary, a preserve, already equipped with a university-run research station, though the station was largely out of commission. Graduate students still stayed there occasionally, and now and then ornithologists and whale researchers. A team of marine ecologists went for initial testing, but their tests had turned up nothing. Perhaps the water was colder, some speculated. Perhaps the particular current that swept around the archipelago kept the disease—if it was disease—from settling in the Dog Island tide pools. Perhaps there was something atypical about the kelp beds just off the island that served as protection. They needed more data. They needed a more functional lab and more time.

This is when Liis got the email from an old colleague. The job: take up residence on the island for a month and manage the initial lab setup there. Make daily documentation of the water, the land, the sea stars. Write a report at the end of her stay. It would be tedious work, which was why no tenured faculty member wanted it. A team was going to be posted on the island, but not until midsummer, when the temperatures might show the most deviation from the norm and therefore be most informative. They needed her merely as a bridge—someone to keep the site from complete shutdown for a month. Would she take it?

Merely as a bridge. She read the line in the email over and over.

Liis was a 48-year-old adjunct professor with a stalled book project on the reproductive decline in marine echinoderms as water temperatures rose. She'd published well fifteen years earlier. At the beginning of her career, she'd even been considered "promising," a researcher to watch.

But then she fell pregnant, left her postdoc, turned down all offers to travel with research teams up to Alaska or across the water to Japan. She vanished herself into another life, domesticity, and she was—unfashionably, unspeakably—happy there.

Now her life was something else again. Her daughter had died in late February 2011. Afterward, grief. When she got the email from her former colleague—one of the few people who knew about Alena—Liis was a year into the dissolution of her marriage. Still sick in love, still deep in grief. She said yes and packed her bag.

The day she left the mainland, she stood on the deck of the ferry and felt the wind rush through her body. Not *at* or *around*, but *through*. She texted her nearly ex-husband: *I'm truly gone now.* And when she could not stop herself, added: *Have I made a huge mistake?*

Three dots appeared and vanished. She waited. Finally, from him: *You'll be okay. This is good.*

Maybe he was right. She was molting one self so that a new skin could harden around her. She shut off the phone and leaned into the force of the wind, letting it hold her upright, a brace.

Two hours later she was on Dog Island, the chartered boat the university had hired to carry her there motoring away from her, a long white tail of wake frothing in the water between her and everything she'd left. She was, she realized, wholly alone for the first time in years. Again she thought, *I've made a mistake.* There was nothing to be done about any of it now. She collected herself and followed her own shadow up the footpath from the dock to the research station, ignoring the terror of her own loneliness, which was, even as she forced herself to dismiss it, already a quiet ticking in her chest, a clock unwinding against time.

Six weeks earlier she'd sat across from her husband at a table in the lobby of the art museum where they'd met twenty years before, asking him what he wanted from her. She'd chosen the location, but not to twist the knife; it was simply their spot, the place they'd come nearly every weekend for coffee. Once she was there, though, she regretted it. The museum had recently been renovated, and the charm of the old version of the building was reduced to the saucer and teacup under her fingers—the last of the former place to survive reconstruction. Now the museum was a cathedral of minimalism, all white walls and vaulted ceilings crested in glass. The wood floors had been stripped to their barest nude and varnished in a clear matte, honed precisely to look unfinished. It was luxury posing as austerity—all the rage in

Seattle. She hated it, and her hatred grew the longer she sat in the space with him. The space, in fact, began to feel like a metaphor for the man, for the life they'd had before. He had changed, he said. The last year—Alena's death—had changed him, and he couldn't be a person he no longer was.

"What does that even mean?"

"I can't tell you more than what I've said."

"But I know you."

"Yes." He put his hand on hers.

"Change is part of it, right? Part of aging. I knew you'd change." She wanted to get up and move around the table to face him, to sit in his lap, to wrap herself around him. A cat. Possessive and feral and demanding. She looked at the other patrons: a woman in a beige wool coat drinking an espresso, an old couple reading a physical newspaper, a young mother in yoga clothes spooning yogurt into the open mouth of a child in a stroller. They'd stare, but what would it matter?

"I'm walking away," he said. "I have to." He said it like it was his only choice, the way to save himself.

"Away from me, you mean," she said.

"Those were the wrong words." He withdrew his hand, balled up his napkin. He was about to leave.

She felt frantic, panicked. Her heart beat arrhythmically in her chest. She forced herself to stay in her seat.

He said, "I shouldn't have said I'm walking away. I mean I need to go forward, Liis. I understand that you're not there yet, and that's fine. But I can't talk about it anymore."

Overhead, tethered to the highest beams of the museum's new ceiling, an installation of papier-mâché birds soared, suspended, their massive white bodies and spread wings throwing arcs of shadow down onto the floor below. She thought about the logistics of raising those bodies from the floor, the impossible weight of something that now looked so weightless. They seemed almost to be wheeling circles up there, in motion. It made her want to close her eyes.

She stood up. "Say good-bye, then," she told him, and they went out to her car, leaving his in the parking lot, and drove to the apartment that had been theirs together but was now only hers, and they got into bed and stayed there until dusk, and there was comfort in those hours. She knew the smell of his skin, the way his scalp felt under her fingers, the way her legs felt around his hips. She knew these things like she had once known her own body, and now both were foreign to her, or she to them. What was that? Grief? Did grief necessarily make an exile of the grieving? She said, "Stay with me," by which she meant both *Don't do this—don't leave,* and also, more literally, *Don't pull out.* And for a few minutes he did stay, and she felt him pulse once, twice, and then just the heat of him close to her before he withdrew and rolled away.

When she returned him to the museum lot to retrieve his car, it was dark, and she said, “We don’t have to do this.”

He was crying. “You’re a ghost,” he said. “You’ve made yourself a ghost.”

A year earlier she might have felt those words, but now, nothing. She nodded and he opened the car door. “I’ll never see you again,” she said.

“That’s not true. You’re being dramatic.”

“I’ll never see you again,” she said again though, and he got in his car and drove away.

Back at the apartment, she called her sister.

“I don’t know what I expected,” Liis said.

“Decency,” her sister answered.

“He’s doing the best he can.”

“I doubt that.”

“He said I’m a ghost.”

Silence. Then, “You are, but it’s not forever. He’s supposed to wait for you to come back.”

“You feel like I’m gone too?”

“You’re coping with a trauma.”

“So the separation is my fault?”

“Look, Liis, you always let him off the hook, even before.”

"I know. Because I love him."

"You have to stop that."

When they hung up, Liis typed in a new text message: *Do you believe in an afterlife? I want to believe. I want to believe we'll see each other there, if never here again.* She left the phone in the bedroom and filled a bath and got into it, let the water lap around the soft mound of her belly, which she once hated but now felt disembodied affection for. It would forever be rounded, never fully submersible again.

The island was small, steep sided, and verdant with spring that first week of her stay. Liis slowly adjusted to the rhythm of its landscape and of her own isolation there. Each morning she woke up to the sunrise and made coffee with the electric kettle and a single-cup filter. She fried an egg on the hot plate that served as a kitchen and ate standing at the window, watching the water go from black to blue to silver white. Water could be light on the island, she learned. It could also be wind or fog or a sheet of tiny diamonds dropped like a towel from the bare flank of a late-morning sky. It twisted and re-formed itself, the same but different.

After eating she dressed and gathered supplies, panted down to the beach for her samples, and then panted as she hiked back up to the station again, breaking a sweat beneath her arms and under her breasts and down the length of her spine. She hadn't moved this much in over a year, and it was strange to feel her body working in service of her will. Her legs were weak beneath her, and only the landscape kept her distracted from the burn in her calves. Under her feet a pelt of moss covered the ground in electric green, and between the spare red bones of the madrone stands, wild rose bushes spotted with fuchsia-colored buds grew in thickets. Small glittering clouds of gnats hung in vibrating sheets here and there. Near each rose bush, bees thrummed, eager, anticipatory. They made the place seem to undulate at times, a disorienting reality that Liis couldn't get used to. And everywhere there was the salt smell of the water, the sound of the tide smashing its face against the rocks, the open-palmed wind gusting up from the water and across the crown of the land.

There were also the gulls. The gulls! Were they always so loud? They called and circled, called and circled. Sometimes they roosted on the peak of the research station, shitting white luminescent streaks down the metal slant of the roof. They bickered and stank. They carried clam shells and blue-black mussels up from the beach and dropped them on the concrete patio just outside Liis's sleeping quarters, splitting them open for their meat. Each day there seemed to be more broken shells. How could the place produce such an abundance? It was as if the moment the gulls scavenged something from the sea floor, a replacement materialized in its place. Sometimes, a school of fish moved through the water near the island and the gulls lifted as one and flew out, seeming to multiply before her eyes, until they had become a churning single organism, a cyclone made of wings that rotated and spun a few feet from shore, one or two birds at a time diving down to pluck a silver body from the water. When this happened, she remembered the museum installation, as if these gulls were an echo of those and all her life was just a net of connections she would never escape. That was a low-moment thought, though.

The practical explanation for the gulls: The island was teeming with life. It was a wildlife sanctuary, which was why the station had been built here. Ornithologists came out each year to track migratory changes. Botanists came to record the effects of the deer on the grasses. Now and then, she'd been told, an artist was permitted a week to photograph or paint the island, which was rough but beautiful, feral and fecund, a little otherworldly. People who'd stayed at the station had recorded waking to the sound of whales exhaling in unison as they passed the shore. The populations of white-tailed deer and red foxes were large here, where there were no predators. There were bald eagles roosting on the sheltered western side of the island, and the rocks at the beach could be overturned to reveal urchins and crabs, anemones in bright orange and pink and spongy green. At night she'd seen opalescent nudibranchs, jellyfish lit ghostly blue, spider crabs creeping the tide pools on their spindly stems like daddy longlegs. They were all relatively safe in this untouched place—even the sea stars, inexplicably. The longer she stayed, the more she began looking for the expected other side of such a place: death. As she walked the game trails, she kept her eyes out for a carcass or the remains of a deer or a fox. The hawks had to drop prey now and then. And where were the bones of those fish she'd seen picked from the water? Where were the bits left to sink into the ground, fertilizer for the roses? She didn't see anything, and the longer she stayed, the more she began to think there was a link she was missing between these other animals and the sea stars. What kept everything alive here? Part of her wondered, illogically, if it truly kept *everything alive.* What could such a possibility mean? She held her phone in her chest pocket where it bumped against her breast as she walked. *What if there were a place where everything lived?* The question tucked itself into her side like a stitch and ached as she walked. She tried to ignore it.

By the end of the first week, she had fallen into a new pattern, waking at daybreak and going about her first collection of the day, spending the late morning and early afternoon testing samples and wandering the island taking notes before returning to the station to sleep until her hunger woke her. She'd eat and go out again, crossing the fields with a lantern and a headlamp. Under her beams the dark fell away and the water burned a bright bottle green. She could see what wasn't visible by daylight: moon snails with their skirted feet out and rippling, tiny schools of flashing fish with yellow eyes. Once she spotted a little octopus, red and cartoonish, bobbing between two rocks. Another time, a flat expanse of anemones open like dahlias beneath the water. And the sea stars! Purple and orange, white and burgundy. There were dozens of them, and every one she saw appeared healthy, thick-limbed, vibrantly fleshed. Each night she scooped water from around them, lifted them gently and scraped the edge of her swab against their bodies.

At the end of the week, having found nothing in her water samples, she selected a dozen stars to bring back to the lab; she would have to test their bodies. All the way back up the hillside, she felt the stars on her back the way she'd have felt a collection of stones weighing down her pack. *Psychic weight*, she thought. She hated to destroy something so beautiful. What could a sea star know about destruction, though? What could anyone know, for that matter, until it happened?

That night, she worked late. She tested the water she'd gathered, recorded her temperature readings from the shoreline, and finally laid out the stars and cut one limb from each. These she dropped into plastic bags, labeling the bags with the stars' names and the coordinates of the locations at which she'd pulled them from the water. She put the arms into the lab's mini freezer. In the morning she'd pack them with ice into a cooler, which she'd take to the dock and leave for the same man who had ferried her out to carry back to the mainland for testing. The maimed stars she would return to the water in the morning too; though for the night, she left them in a bucket of seawater and then dropped into her sleeping bag. Just before she slept, she reached for her phone. Like a window to another place and time, it lit up a small, bright square in the darkness. She typed *I wish I could hold you*, then shut off the phone and fell asleep.

Alena's death is the black hole at the center of everything. A Charybdis. It spins and sucks, infinite in its desire to pull Liis down. She can only walk to the lip of its churning. If she stays too long there, she'll dive in and let herself drown in it.

What came before it is hard to remember, not because Liis can't recall it, but because it hurts.

What happened following Alena's death though, she lays bare for herself again and again, scouring the past as if the work will rub it smooth of scars.

First, there were months of crying, then months of yelling, then months of silence.

For a while there was a therapist—a short woman with cropped hair the color of cornsilk and eyes that drooped at their outer corners in a way that made her appear pitying, patronizing. She made recommendations and let them talk, first Thomas and then Liis, because if Liis began, Thomas never got his turn.

Liis could be uncontrollable in her grief, and it was unmooring for him. She had always been measured, clear-headed, even calculating. She was a scientist, for fuck's sake. Thomas said this, and Liis looked at him, bewildered by his anger and his misreading of her.

This wasn't true, she said. She'd never been any of those things. Or, no—that wasn't true either. She'd never been clearheaded, never measured. Calculating, maybe. Controlled, certainly. There was a difference between what one felt and what one showed of those feelings, wasn't there? There was an inner and an outer self. But the barrier between the two had been weakened by Alena's death. Everything in her that was a mess—she couldn't hide it. And he shouldn't ask her to.

No, he said. No. Maybe he shouldn't, but he didn't know how to hold it all for himself and her too. That was the problem. She wanted to grieve forever, like it would keep Alena with them. She wanted to let her grief infect their whole lives forever.

You're wrong, she told him. It wounded her to hear him say it as he had: *infect*. As if her sorrow was a poison and not their shared love inverted. Isn't that what Alena had been—the manifestation of their shared love? How could he not see that grief was simply the same love turned inside out? That grief was the shadow that love had left behind? What Liis wanted now was for time to move backward. She wanted a do-over. She wanted to wake up one morning and find that none of it had really happened at all.

They argued in quiet, even tones, which the therapist said was healthy—an airing. But as much as they aired it all, nothing was repaired, and Liis left the sessions feeling as if she had held her head over a toilet for an hour and come out empty of everything, exhausted. It was she who ended their appointments.

After that there was a dinner one night just after Thomas finally moved out. He'd found an apartment for himself across the city—a studio, tiny and spare and too sad for Liis to bear considering as his living space. He didn't care though. For a few weeks, he seemed to have vanished wholly, and then out of nowhere he texted her about meeting. Liis's stomach sank at the invitation, which she assumed he was arranging in order to tell her that he'd begun dating again, that he wanted to divorce. But it wasn't that. *I miss you*, he said in his text. Could they grab a meal together?

They ate at their old restaurant—not one where they'd taken Alena, but one they went to together, on date nights. They had a bottle of wine, and he reached for her hand as they left, suggesting they walk the pier near the apartment, like they'd always done. It was Liis who kissed him—a risk, but also nothing after twenty years of kisses. How strange, that duality. She said it aloud after she pulled away from him. *What is this? Not a first kiss, but not familiar.* He laughed and kissed her again. He went home with her, to their home, and it wasn't until the morning that she realized he hadn't slept there but had waited for her to sleep and then left. It felt like a trick. If he'd stayed the night, she would have been hopeful about the future, but because he'd left, the whole evening became an uncertainty. Suddenly the dinner wasn't about reconnection but about her loneliness. The sex she'd thought was good was now merely nostalgic. And she—she was not desirable, the love of his life returned to him. No. She was foolish. A fool. There was a note on the counter: *Thank you for a nice evening*, it read. So neutral. She balled it up and threw it out.

But he called again the next week, and the following one too, and each time she said yes and met him for dinner and then brought him home—for sex, or sex and a movie, or just a movie sometimes—as if the easy companionship between them had returned. Each time he declined to stay too long, pulling on his coat and going back to his own apartment to sleep, walking away from her again and again. Some mornings the apartment smelled of him—his pillow, the sheets—but other than that there was no trace of him, and a part of her wondered if she was imagining it all. Was it possible that Thomas had never come back into her life after the separation but that she—somehow—was losing her grip on the veil between fantasy and reality? Could you want a thing enough to trick yourself into believing you had it? Was she losing her mind? She remembered stories she'd read of women with phantom pregnancies, or veterans with pain in limbs long ago amputated from their bodies, or states of psychosis that enabled a person to slide from one personality to another. It could happen. This terrified her.

Her sister said she was being melodramatic and ridiculous. "He's using you because he can't figure out what he wants," her sister said. "That's what's happening. Stop seeing him, Liis."

"You can't understand. Everything you have is still intact."

The truth was that she didn't want to stop, though. She'd rather have a spectral marriage than no marriage at all.

In the morning the walk to the beach to return the stars was slow, the bucket heavy with their bodies and the water, where they clung to one another in a heap. Liis paused to breathe and to look out across the stretch of silver gray to the other islands just visible in the distance: Lucia and Varg. There was a strangeness to the landscape this morning, a dreaminess. Fog had rolled in overnight—a marine layer—and it lay in an opaque band a foot above the water's surface. Behind it the western horizon was still deep and silty gray. The fog had socked in the air rather than letting wind move freely around the island, and Liis descended to the sea through the heavy smell of salt and mineral. On the beach itself, a great raft of driftwood was banked against the cliff wall, and swaths of green and red kelp hung from the logs. She hadn't been wakened by the sounds of a storm, but the evidence of massive waves and wind was everywhere, as if the sea floor had been churned upward and left to dry on the sand.

She was squatted at the waterline, about to withdraw a star from the bucket to place between the rocks, when the phone in her pocket chimed. It hadn't done that since she'd come out to the island. There was no service here, and her only way to call out had been the radio. None of her own texts had sent. But she paused and took out her phone and looked at it. *I wish I could hold you*, the screen read. It was her own words from the night before come back to her. But also, no—these weren't exactly her words. Her outgoing message hung above these words, still protected in its green bubble. These words sat below it, not enclosed, but free-floating, just type on the screen face, gray and faint. A glitch, she told herself, and dropped it back in her pocket, went about her work.

For the rest of the morning she felt trailed by the sensation that something had slipped through the veil. As she walked around the island, she felt the phone bouncing against her leg. When she left the cooler of iced sea star arms on the eastside dock, she asked the private boat's pilot if he got reception out here. He was a craggy-faced man in his late 50s, his gray hair tied back in a ponytail.

"I don't carry a phone," he said. "A radio, fine. But no phone." His face split in a rough grin. "Who'd call me?" A grizzled laugh, and he stepped into his swaying boat and waved over his shoulder as he left her alone again.

All day she worried it, an idea slowly taking shape in her mind.

A memory: She is standing at the kitchen window, washing the dinner dishes. It's the blue hour, late winter. Thomas is in his backyard studio, finishing the day's work. He has a new series in mind: ten large-scale paintings in cyan and gold and black, abstract but reminiscent of the nets that light and shadow cast on water. Each canvas will be slightly different than the others, but mounted together, they'll form a wall of water. He's excited about the project in a way he hasn't been about any of his work for quite some time, and she's happy for him. Happy to see him lit up from the inside—his capacity for generating his own sense of purpose something she most admires in him. She has always used him like a flare, following his light while her own falters, unsteady, leaving her aimless in her own life.

Tonight, she can see him in silhouette through the fogged studio window, and her love for him feels immense, overpowering. She can never admit this to him—that she loves him so boundlessly, so lavishly. She can never tell him that she thinks she'd die without him. That without him she knows she'd atrophy and become nothing. It's repellant to her, this dependence. It's shameful. And beyond that, it'd be too much for him to hold. But watching the shape of him through the window, she has to will herself to stay in place so that she doesn't run out across the dark lawn in her bare feet to embrace him.

She's thinking this when there's a call. She fishes her phone from her pocket with still-wet hands, catching it on the last ring.

"Liis." It's Alena's coach.

Her memory of the next hour is punctured with great holes through which only pain is visible.

Liis did run to Thomas in the studio. Together, they rushed to the high school pool. Alena had hit her head during a dive, swallowed water, and been pulled unconscious to the tile deck. The coach had done CPR, and she'd come to, vomited. Liis and Thomas pulled up just as the paramedics were loading Alena into the ambulance. The other parents watched as Liis climbed in beside her daughter. They were going to take their own wet-headed children home and feed them and go to bed knowing all was well. Liis thought this as the ambulance doors closed on her.

The hospital. Waiting. Fluorescent lights and smells of disinfectant, sickness, coffee. One doctor and another, pulling Liis and Thomas aside. A bed in a room in the ER, followed by an MRI, followed by a bed in the trauma unit. A nurse with close-cropped hair and a warm hand. A nurse with a tight ponytail and a sharp tone. A nurse. A nurse. A nurse. Liis's sister arrived and sat with her but left at eight o'clock to return to her own children and her husband. Impossible to think that their nighttime routine was carrying on as usual, though the world had stopped.

At midnight Liis, who had been dozing in the chair beside Alena's hospital bed, woke to the machines in the room all screaming and Alena blue-lipped on the bank of white pillows. Alena's hand was still in Liis's, their fingers interlaced.

And then it was over.

Unthinkable.

Everything else can only be Afterward.

She spends the month following Alena's death under her own kind of water. It laps at her and tugs her deeper. In March, from the screen of her laptop, she sits in bed in her darkened bedroom watching footage of the Tōhoku earthquake and tsunami. She cannot stop watching. "A seismic rupture," she hears a reporter say, and the words dislodge something in her gut that comes up in the form of sobs. When Thomas finds her, she is on the bedroom floor.

Later, in May, his series of paintings is finished, and he exhibits at a gallery he has been trying to get into for years. He is a wild success. A glowing review runs in the paper ahead of the opening. The gallery owner orders a crate of champagne.

When Liis walks into the gallery, she sees the work before she sees her husband. What he said months before comes back to her: a wall of water. She staggers forward. The wall is at the back of a wide and empty room. The space is flooded with white light. Standing in front of it, Liis closes her eyes. She sees the riotous brilliance of one of her memory holes, but this time she steps through it, and when she opens her eyes again, she is inches from the blue wave of Thomas's paintings. She gasps.

When they finally go to therapy, Thomas will tell the placid therapist about this night and how Liis left before the champagne was served, how he spent the evening worrying about where she'd gone and if she was okay. How he could not be present in the moment, a professional peak. He is not a bad man. This is not about his ego. He was anxious when he should have been celebrating. Liis will apologize. The wall of water will pool between them.

Where had she gone? the therapist will wonder aloud, but Liis won't be able to tell her.

"I walked," she'll say, which will be true, though she won't be sure where she walked or how she ended up across the city, on the westside point, looking out at Puget Sound and its rippling darkness, the whole of the water spotted with reflected lights that seemed to shine both from beyond and from beneath. "How could that be?" Liis will ask the therapist, and the poor woman will turn her pitying face to Thomas and nod.

On the island she waited for dusk, stowed a lantern and her dinner in her pack, and hiked down to the beach.

The tide was low but beginning to come back in, and the pools between the rocks were exposed. When she shone the lantern beam at her feet, it illuminated a garden of anemones and limpets, quarter-sized crabs, sea stars. Liis pulled her phone from her pocket. To Alena's number, she texted, *Where are you?*

For several minutes she stood with the phone in her hand, waiting. When the sun fully slid into the sea, she sat and ate her meal and watched the phone.

Around her the pools crackled and whispered.

Still nothing on the phone.

She pulled up Thomas's number and typed, *I think she's looking for me. I think she's found me out here on the island.* Send. A moment later, a chime that made her heart stop, but it was just the error message. Nothing could get through to Thomas.

It occurred to her to put her feet in the water. If the water was truly regenerative, special, it may be contact that mattered. She had her hands in it on the first day. She touched the water, and then she touched her phone. This seemed logical. She stripped to bare feet and climbed past the tide pools to a flat section of rock. The lip of the incoming tide licked her feet.

The water was frigid. Again, part of her mind wondered at this—the chill here and how the water around the island seemed to remain cooler than farther north.

Disease in the stars would spread more quickly in warmer temperatures, where the creatures' systems were already stressed. Climate change and toxicity and plague, they were bedfellows, no different from grief and depression and divorce. One crisis would always beget another. There were no isolated events.

As she waited she remembered the videos of the Tōhoku tsunami—the way the whole of the sea drew away from the land as if sucking in its breath before letting loose a fury. She'd read somewhere that the tsunami waves had come at the coastline as fast as five miles per second and ruined centuries of development in a single wash. What was remarkable about disasters was not just their interconnection (the shifting plates, the shaking land, the flood) but also the way they collapsed time, folding it on itself, making clear the reality that the past is always present, and the present is a long coil of return. If there was any barrier between this world and whatever lay beyond it, that barrier was time. Wherever there was forward motion, destruction and ruin would come again, and with them, also, a new beginning. Time was a cycle. A cyclone. A whirlpool. And nothing living could escape its turning.

Although, she thought, Thomas had.

She texted him: *How could you put all your grief into the paintings? How could you do that?* She resented him.

She acknowledged it to herself as she hadn't before. She resented the way he'd pulled away from her after Alena was gone, which he'd done so naturally, not a seam between their daughter's disappearance and his work's emergence. The day after her death, he was in the studio. He was there early in the mornings and late into the night. All the hours while Liis was in the bedroom watching tsunami footage and reliving that night in the hospital, Thomas was in the studio working. Compelled. Focused. Creating. She resented that the energy of their shared grief had become productive for him—a birth—while for her it had been a force of wreckage.

The text sat in its bubble, unanswered. A failure message chimed. Liis put on her shoes and began up the cliffside.

The act of remembering that night is never intentional. Memory forces itself through her consciousness like a headache. The holes in what she recalls appear first—bright, excruciating blasts of light at the backs of her eyes that wake her from deep sleep or hit her when she's passed Alena's closed bedroom door. Sometimes a memory begins not with light but with sound—a roaring like a train through her skull. She wakes up shaking, deaf to anything but the rumbling. There's an ache, as if her joints are grinding against themselves with the rupture of what she's submerged. She fights this, but once a memory is moving, she has to wait for it to wash over and through her. Sometimes she has to lie down on her back to resist the vertigo, the nausea, of remembering. It's incapacitating. Thomas doesn't know how to help her. He brings her Alena's pillow, which for weeks after her death still smells like her. This helps until it doesn't. Then he lays his own body beside hers, curling himself around her, but how long can they stay inert? He asks this finally: *How long, Liis?* Finally, he's gone, and she must weather these moments alone, and maybe this is better. Without him she has no choice but to give in to the flood. One lesson of grief is submission.

Back at the station, she packed in near darkness, emptying and cleaning the lab equipment, locking the cabinets, sweeping the sand from the floor with only the light of her lantern casting a sallow haze over the lab. In the sleeping quarters, she filled her backpack with her clothes and notebook and toiletries—a life could be reduced to so little. Her mouth tasted like metal—had she bitten herself?—and so she went out into the night with her toothbrush and water bottle and brushed and spat into the tall grass. All around her the island hushed and chittered. The gulls were quieted at night, but the insects hummed their nocturnal songs, and the rising tide threw itself against the beach. Liis stood still in the center of it all—the darkness and the noise. The violence and the return. Overhead, stars like punctures in the sky. Below, the black varnish of the sea. She could, she knew, walk to the edge of the eastern side of the island and jump. The cold would kill her before she drowned, and that death would not be so miserable—an initial shuddering, then lethargy. She thought of the scenes from Tōhoku—the detritus of so many lives slopping and bobbing in the flood waters. Couches and beds. Automobiles and dining tables and the soft, indistinguishable lumps of fabric that might have been winter coats or bedroom curtains or the backs of the drowned.

She knew she wouldn't be able to dive into the sea. She couldn't explain how she belonged on this side any more than she could explain how her daughter belonged on the other, but she understood that the passage across their divide was an impossibility.

She went into the station and shut off the lantern and lay on the floor to wait for morning, when she would radio the private boat pilot to come get her. She was done here. She would write the report from home. She would use it to negotiate herself a new adjunct post in the university's lab, perhaps. Or maybe not that. Maybe she would sell the apartment but not go anywhere, just stay with her sister until she knew what should come next. Until she knew where to go, now that she'd washed up on the shore of her life once more. Maybe she would sell the apartment and travel. There were sea stars to be studied in Canada, in Mexico. One way or another, she had no choice but to begin again.

The station was cold and silent, and she felt herself lift out of her body and hover like a gull riding the channel of wind between waking and sleeping. She named the losses: *Pisaster ochraceus, Pisaster giganteus, Pisaster Brevispinus, Filia Alena, Amatus Thomas*. Almost a prayer. They passed behind her eyes, bright blossoming flares—beautiful—and then vanished. Into the phone her fingers typed: *I miss you. What am I going to do?*

The words rose and hung on the screen.

At the Last

At the last, Otto reconsiders. Maybe everybody does. The only benefit of aging is getting smarter about yourself. But the smarter you get, the more you question your past. On this day he wakes with a flurry of questions. A host of them. A chorus. (*There ought to be a better word for it*, he thinks. *A hallelujah.* Yes—he has a hallelujah of questions.) He lies on his back looking up at the blue light glazing the ceiling of his bedroom. *Out of the blue,* he thinks. And then: *Is anything ever really out of the blue?*

He narrows his eyes so that the light in the room wobbles, darkens. *Blue bird. Blue blood. Blue eyes. Blue sea.* Through the window, though, the world is black and white. Hard stillness of the bare treetops. Milk-white weight of the sky. The temperature has fallen. He thinks of the lake near the parsonage where he grew up, on the other side of the Cascade Mountains. Winters there froze your eyelashes and sent spores of cold feathering into your lungs after each breath. Otto recalls the hiss of an ice skate blade cutting across the surface of that frozen lake, the chill like a bruise at the back of his neck where his coat gaped from his skin. The ache of warming up again after a long, dark day in the worst weather.

God, yes, he thinks, rolling over, setting his feet on the floor. *That warming up—how it burned.*

He sits on the edge of the bed until the world orients itself for him, then maneuvers himself into some clothes, takes the stairs slow. In the kitchen the calendar over the coffeepot tells him it's January the twenty-eighth. There's a big red X over the day's box. *Yes, today*, he thinks. *It's today.* He has a tendency to lose track of the days now that there's nothing structuring them, nothing keeping one from weeping into the next. The effect of this seepage of time is actually counterintuitive, though: It's speed.

"Today is January the twenty-eighth," he says out loud, the pitch of disbelief in his voice. He wants to hear himself say it so that it registers, else in an hour he'll be surprised again. He counts the remaining days of this month—*onetwothreefour*—in a single breath, flips the page. Picture of a blue glacier, slug of electric-blue water, flourish of some kind of arctic wildflower like a little river of white stars against the white snow. It was his little granddaughter, Anders's youngest girl, 7 years old, who sent him this calendar back at Christmas. Saskia is her name. She chose the calendar for her grandfather herself, her father reported. It's twelve months of photos of wild Alaska.

"Why Alaska?" Otto had asked over the phone, and the girl had just giggled.

"Why Alaska, Sas?" he repeated.

The long pause of her thinking. "Because, Pop," she said. "Because why not?"

"Yes, why not?" he'd said. "That's a good reason."

How he'd felt the pins and needles beneath his skin all the rest of that day. *Why not? Why not? Why not?* His granddaughter had jarred something loose in him. Had he forgotten that question? He thought he had. Somewhere in the swallow of the last few years, he had forgotten the *why not.*

Now, he waits at the counter while the coffee drips. He fries himself a single egg, which he lays carefully on a piece of dry toast, yellow eye up. He eats sitting at the table by the window, looking at the stretch of the property he bought after he left his marriage and came out here alone to this island—twelve years ago, though it feels like half that, or one quarter. In his head he is still new to this place, still figuring it out. In his head he is not 86, but 60. And he'd like to be even younger—40, maybe, or even 25.

He'd like back that sweep of still-straw-colored hair on his head, that thirty-two-inch waist, that hum in his center that might be called desire. He'd like to start again and again and again.

For a second he can almost feel it, too. He cuts into his egg, and it is as creamy as Easter morning on his tongue. He downs a swig of his coffee, and it is strong and black and wakes him up.

This is another thing about aging, though: that live-wire feeling never lasts long anymore. Once his plate is clean, he cannot conjure the drive to get up. His legs are leaden. His chest is heavy. So he sits and looks out the window.

It strikes him that it's not just him. Nothing is awake to the point of desire in January. There's comfort in that. At least this morning, there's a companionable silence coming from the woods. The pines and cedars that border his yard are quieted, all tipped with frost and the strict winter light. The bare deciduous skeletons of the alders and the birches and the maples stand rigidly still. And far off, like a shingle on the horizon, the sea is a solid strip of gray.

"What do you do out there all day, Dad?" his daughter asked all those years ago when he first moved out here on his own. He'd heard the soup of worry and resentment in her voice. He'd heard all her unspoken reservations about his age, the distance, his solitude.

How could he confess that he liked to sit at the window and stare out? That this particular inactivity could keep him for hours, for whole mornings some days? It would have confirmed all her doubts.

"I'm fine, you know. I'm not the old man you think I am."

"I don't think that." She was too quick on return; he'd hit the right fear.

"There's plenty to keep busy with here. I won't get bored."

"I'm not worried about bored."

"I won't get lonely."

Silence.

"I promise you. And, anyhow, loneliness is cathartic."

One of the old islanders had told him that the phone company had run the cables under the sea to get them out here, and though he was dubious, he had imagined his words like slim fish swimming through the deepwater lines to her on the mainland, silver, peaceful, true.

But the other truth was that she hadn't been entirely wrong to worry. He'd come to the island under a freeze of darkness. He'd just left his marriage and home, his teaching job. He was reconsidering it all, but also sinking. How had he not known before that loneliness could turn virus? That it could slow your thoughts in the same way cold slows the movement of water until that water becomes ice. He hadn't before thought of ice and darkness as belonging together. Ice is bright, white, beautiful. But that vision was ignorant. In the months after the divorce, when he moved out here to the island, he understood that at the bottom of everything is absence. Absence of heat. Absence of light. Absence of desire. Absence of love. His father, had he lived that long, would have looked at him with shame and said that what he needed was God—that he'd turned away from God, and that was the absence he felt. *Better to be absent from the body and at home with the Lord.* But there's no way to truly absent yourself from your own body. Or, rather, no way to absent yourself from the absences you feel in your body. Loneliness like a bruise that bleeds from the soft tissues of the gut to the surface of the skin and goes cold there. Apathy like a swelling weight in every limb. Head a frozen cloud. Silence growing like ice in the cave of his mouth. And at the pit of him, darkness, deep and galactic cold.

On some nights he stood at the same window where he stands now, unmoving, watching night fall. First the dark line of the sea bled into the lip of the sky, and then it traveled up and up, until the whole expanse—all he could see beyond the glass in front of his nose—was a liquid blue-black.

It's Chaos, he'd think. Nyx and Hemera, battling again. Darkness as the result of a celestial violence. And later, when dawn ripped the same sky head to tail with a slice of gray light, he would reconsider: *But light is violence too.*

What a lot of sentiment, he thinks now. What a lot of poetic bullshit. He's still prone to it, even now. He can't help himself.

He hears his father's voice at the back of his head: *For we wrestle not against flesh and blood, but against the darkness of this world.*

Otto shakes his head. Enough. He has to get up, do something, fill this day. He gets into his coat and hat and makes his way out to the car. It takes several minutes to warm the engine enough for the clouds on the windows to evaporate, and when he gets behind the wheel, his breath is visible. "Ha," he says, normal volume at first, watching the word take the shape of a puff. Then, "HA!" Big plume. He waves it away.

On the road into town, he passes fields and bogs and the manicured geometries of people's fenced-in yards. The frost has flattened the grass, turned it waxy brown. A fawn-colored rabbit manifests suddenly from what a second before was ordinary ground and leaps ten feet in front of the car. Otto swerves, swears, goes on.

In the sheep pasture near the firehouse, the animals stand in a cluster looking dumbly at the road, all their black faces following the car as it approaches and moves off.

In the hay field beyond that, the wheels of alfalfa spun in the summer have been blanketed for the season in white plastic. They're giant marshmallows against the cream of sky, surreal and glittering a sheen of frost.

In town Otto pulls into a spot in front of the grocery store. He needs—what? He sits in the car, willing his mind to move a little faster, but nothing comes to him. He should have written it down.

In the store he walks the short aisles looking, hoping whatever it was he meant to buy will call to him when he sees it. Beans? Lettuce? Oranges? Wine? Yes—always wine. He puts a bottle of red and a bottle of white into his cart. Also, a bag of onions and a bag of potatoes, a sack of bread, a jar of imported lingonberry jam—very expensive, but worth it—and a paper-wrapped bundle of fish fillets. He's hungriest for these things his mother made—plain boiled vegetables, pickles, fish, good bread. He doesn't taste as sharply as he once did, but it's more than that; it's comfort. Or maybe just retreat. Aging is time moving swiftly forward and backward at once. Chaos, never truly ordered. He is a fish in a bowl, swimming round and round and thinking every pass is new.

He has a memory of his ex-wife eating his mother's pickled fish one Christmas when they were newly married—Ilse with her oversensitive tongue and her superior gag reflex. Her face contorted at the first bite.

Her cheeks flushed. When his mother turned away, she'd taken his glass of scotch and drained it to the ice cubes, drowning the briny taste.

At the time Otto had laughed. Later, when he was looking for them, he saw it as a sign of their mismatch, his people never really her people. Now he thinks middle age overcomplicated everything for him. If he could wish back one aspect of youth, it would be the simplicity with which he received the world as a younger man. It was all still glittering then. All worth laughing at or swallowing or fucking. All of it. He'd like to fill with desire that way again—any desire—even if only for a moment.

At the checkout he asks, "What day is this?"

The girl behind the counter is the big, dark-haired daughter of the store's owner. Otto has been on-island long enough both to know this and to remember her as a little child. She's probably almost 20 now, this girl, this woman. She frowns at him. "The twenty-eighth," she says.

"Right," Otto says.

"You okay?" She eyes him. He remembers her with black pigtails, cherubic cheeks. Today she wears her hair short and has colored it blue.

Interesting choice, Otto thinks. "Interesting choice," he says aloud.

The woman frowns. "You okay? You alone here, or someone's with you?"

"I mean your hair. I'm fine."

She looks at him. "Okay," she says, dismissive, and hands him his receipt.

As he leaves, he turns her question over in his mind *You okay?* No verb. Or *okay* the verb. *Okay* as a form of *to be*. A state of being, neither active nor passive. Existing. *You okay out here alone? You existing?*

He thinks of his daughter. She worries about this. How's his safety? His sanity? His heart? She is a flurry of anxieties. *Are you okay out there, Dad? Are you still okay to be left alone? When will you reconsider your living situation?* That's how she always puts it—his *situation*—as if he is an armchair, misplaced to the wrong corner of the room. To the wrong house.

"This situation," he says as he backs the car out of its spot and pulls again onto the road. *From the Latin* sitauatio. *Meaning placement. Meaning location.* He thinks: *I am a fish in a bowl.* Glassy bubbles rise from his mouth, bump against the windshield.

He makes a turn through downtown. The shops all have the closed-up look of the off-season. No tourists come out here to the island in the winter, and he's grateful for the quiet of their absence. For the absence of the quiet. For the shuttering. Hibernation. He turns by the school, where the lights are on behind the windows. What day is it? *January the twenty-eighth. MondayTuesdayWednesday.* People are at their weekday tasks. Is this Monday? He thinks so. The clock on the dash says 11:58. Morning spilling into afternoon. He looks up—sky like snow. Morning splitting open the middle of the day with its soft gray light. It moves and he is static, floating between here and there. He is in situ. He is *in situation normal all fucked up.* This makes him grin as he winds around a wide bend in the road. Dun-colored hillside. Sky meeting grass meeting mud meeting road. One turn after the next. Chorus of hillsides, singing him forward toward the sea, the sea, the sea. On the island every movement is always toward the sea.

And then there it is, that sea—dark bottle green and matte, the usual glitter roughed out with the motion of the wind. Scrubbed with winter, the waves granulated with the churning of their salt.

His father's voice again: *And He overthrew all those cities, and all the inhabitants of those cities, and what grew on the ground.*

He thinks, *Pillars of salt. Pillars of salt. Look backward too long, and you'll cry yourself a pillar of salt.*

He swings the car into the beach lot, brakes more abruptly than he intends. He feels winded suddenly. His parking job is terrible, lopsided. His limbs feel jangled. Jangly. Jittering. *God.*

He reclines the driver's seat. He needs just a minute's rest.

Sometimes, when the weather is bearable, he gets out and walks this beach with bare feet, like a boy again. He fills his coat pockets with fragments of rubbed glass and whorled brown whelk shells to send in envelopes to his granddaughter.

Sometimes, sitting here at the edge of this cold water, he remembers a warmer beach across the world. Years ago. A tiny town on the Mediterranean. A sea the color of a clear glass jar. They took a bus, he and Ilse and the children. (The children were still children then.) They stopped at a beachside bakery and bought cans of soda and a loaf of meringue studded with pistachios. *Pistache*, the sign in the bakery said. *Like mustache*, Otto remembers saying, and his little daughter laughed. They took their lunch to the beach and lay on a blanket in the sand. The children played at the water's edge. He took in the blue sky—*cerulean*, he remembers thinking. Such an odd word. Full of pomp. Full of beautiful sound—*cerulean blue.* Like an echo chamber. He could taste the words. He could taste the air, so full of salt. Ilse's mouth tasted like salt when he kissed her, and when he pulled away, he felt jangled, loose-jointed. Jolted. *That was desire*, he thinks now—desire for more of that thick blue sky, more of his wife's body against his own. *More days exactly like this one. Or that one, rather*, he thinks. He opens his eyes, sees this white sky. He's getting muddled. The usual divisions of time are washing out. And it's infuriating, really. It's infuriating! Where he loses time, he loses reality. He drifts. He lets the fragments of his memories sift and reassemble. He uses his imagination to fill their gaps. And where his imagination diverges from reality, there is inevitable betrayal.

He closes his eyes again.

And then, out of the blue: *You've betrayed me.* His wife's voice this time. No—his ex-wife's voice. Ilse's voice.

How did he tell her he was leaving? He can't remember—not in detail.

It wasn't an impulse—that much is true, even if it might have appeared differently to Ilse.

Out of the blue, she'd said when he told her. *Why would you spring this on me out of the blue?*

It's a funny phrase, Otto has always thought—*out of the blue.* He assumed for years that it referred to falling—catastrophe or surprise dropping down on you, plummeting from the blue width of the sky like a bird. A buzzard arrived to pick your bones clean, or maybe a dove, holy and full of the Pentecostal flames of change. *And there appeared to them tongues of fire, cloven, and they alighted on their heads.* But now it makes much more sense to him to think of the blue as a deep night, an abyss, an absence. Chaos, far down and cold and too dark to see into. And then out of this—suddenly—certainty! Solid and brittle and flashing. Burning and cold. A splinter of ice through the gut. A tongue of ice, fated to melt.

"I don't want to be married," Otto had said. No matter what Ilse believed, the acknowledgement had been a long time coming.

This was October. This was twelve years ago. He was 74. The leaves had just begun to flame out and drop. He had taken Ilse to lunch at a café downtown. He'd looked at her across the table and could barely eat his food. She told a story about finding the neighbor's cat under the car when she'd gone to start it that morning. What if she'd not noticed it? What if she'd just pulled out? She had her fork raised over her plate as she spoke—suspended—and he kept willing her in his mind to set it down. *Set it down.* He couldn't tell her there, in public. They paid the check and left.

Afterward, he drove her to the waterfront. He'd do it there. The sky was high and white that day—just like this one. The water was a sheet of glare. He couldn't look out the windshield at it without squinting. He rolled down the windows just enough to let the cool inside.

"I don't want to be married anymore," he said, and it was done, just like that. *Hallelujah.*

"I don't want to be married anymore." Is that how he said it? Or was it the harder, the more particular, "I don't want to be married *to you* anymore"? He doesn't remember.

On the way back home that day, after he told her, he had needed to pull to the side of the road so she could be sick. Her whole undigested lunch pooled on the gravel shoulder of the road. She retched and retched again, and Otto got out and walked around the car and tried to hold back her hair, but Ilse slammed her elbow into his chest. "Don't touch me," she had said. "You do this to me after a whole lifetime? You do not touch me." She'd wiped her mouth on her sleeve and got back in the car.

How did he say it?

I've been asleep, and I want to wake up. I'm waking up.

No. How did he say it?

I desire something else. I desire desire. Something else out there is desire.

No.

I loved you. I did. I love you.

What would it matter, really, to remember? The moment of the split is not the divorce, just as the moment of union is not the marriage.

What does it matter if you meant to live without breaking things? If you meant to step gently? What conflicting impulses are these—gentleness and desire! They can't live in one body peacefully. They never coexist well.

What has lasted is the image of Ilse as she looked that afternoon in October, sitting beside him in the car, her red hair fallen forward over her face, her hands over her mouth.

Out of the blue, she said, and it took Otto years to understand that what she was really asking him was *How could you do this to me?*

Out of the blue, she kept saying, but all he could hear was the pump of his own blood in his chest, thunderous, like water running again under ice. Like he'd been holding his breath for far too long. Like every suture of flesh holding his ribs together was splitting apart. And he could breathe deeply again.

Now, in the car, he is cold, tired. He could almost sleep. Clouds pass in the sky behind his eyelids. He imagines himself as a little boy crossing the yard behind the parsonage, passing the brick building of the church, running the length of the hay field beyond that. Running, running, heart in his throat, heat of exertion burning in his chest. Where's he going? He tries to see it in his memory. Brown, wet grass. Winter grass. White clumps of melting snow at the base of each tree. And up ahead, a silver slash in the landscape—the lake. He's running to the lake.

Dad! he hears.

He reaches the lake's edge. His breath is a cloud in front of his face. His cheeks are hot. He presses his boot gently on the plate of ice lipping the lake. Bubbles. A visible flush of water rising. The melt seeping into the softening ice.

Dad! he hears again.

And then he can't hold back the impulse to smash it. He stomps. A crack.

Dad?

Freezing water fills his boot.

Otto turns toward the window and opens his eyes. His daughter is standing on the other side of the glass, her face a welt of worry.

After that there's no more slipping. Sylvie has come, as she said she would. Red X on the calendar. Today's the day. She's angry at him for leaving the house when he knew she was coming. "Didn't you remember I was coming?" she says. He worried her, being gone when she arrived at the house. She had to drive all over the island looking for him.

"It's not such a bad place to take a drive," he says.

"Dad," she says, "please don't make this day harder."

She makes him get into her car at the beach, says she'll retrieve his car later. "Or Anders will. I've convinced him to come with me today. I thought you'd like us both with you."

Otto sighs as he fastens his seat belt. Both of his children, come for him. It shouldn't feel like a betrayal.

"I thought you said you wouldn't be driving anymore, anyhow." She looks over her shoulder, backs out of her spot in the beach lot. "I thought you understood that it's not safe for you anymore. You promised."

"How could I get groceries otherwise?" As soon as he says it, he remembers the bag in the trunk of his car, the fish in its package. So be it. Let the car stink to high heaven. Let his son deal with that bit of inconvenience when he comes back for the car. Let this day be a little difficult for the two of them.

At the house his son is waiting. There's a suitcase and a cardboard box near the front door. "Dad," he says. His voice cracks.

"You packed my books?" Otto asks. He looks at the box, tries to imagine what his son would believe he might need. How could he get it right?

"Whatever we've missed, we can come back for later. There won't be a lot of space in your new room, but if you miss something, we'll bring it to you. You just have to tell us," Sylvie says. She's all efficiency, whisking through the front room, checking that the lamps are off. Disappearing into the kitchen, where he can hear her clattering the dishes from the drying rack in the sink to the cupboards. She is her mother's daughter in so many ways, responsible to the end. Responsibility as a way to fake control over the uncontrollable. Where he was desire, Ilse was always control. Or, rather, control was her desire, and his was desire itself. A conflict from the very start, though they couldn't see it at the beginning. At the beginning they seemed to complement each other, to balance. Sky and sea, they thought they were. And that wasn't wrong.

Sylvie bustles out, her face set, her purse slung over her shoulder. "Ready," she says to Anders, not to him.

"I don't want this, you know," Otto says. "I know that doesn't change it, but I need to tell you. I don't want this."

His children say nothing.

For a moment they all stand still, looking at one another. The light in the room is stale, flat, headed toward dusk.

Chaos, he thinks.

Sylvie crosses the room and draws the curtains over the big window. A sheet of shadow falls across the floor.

What would Ilse say if she were here? Ilse, all reason and brusque practicality. *We've aged. We're on the other side now, and that's all there is to it.*

"Where's your mother?" Otto asks.

"Christ," Anders says. "Let's get him to the car."

Sylvie drives. Anders sits beside him in the back, looking pummeled. There are silver-gray circles below his eyes.

"You need to sleep," Otto says, and pats his son's knee.

"I'm okay, Dad." Anders gives him a half smile.

At the ferry they just make the cut, pulling on last, just as the neon-vested attendant waves the line closed. There's a *thump* as the blocks are set behind the back wheels of the car.

"You want to go up?" Sylvie asks. "I could use coffee. Or something. I feel weary."

"I should've brought a flask," Anders says.

"I wish you had." She looks back in the rearview mirror, and Otto catches her eyes. Exhausted look of apology, duty.

"I can't be in this car," Otto says.

They get out. Anders helps him into his coat, keeps a hand on his back as he takes the narrow metal stairs one step at a time up to the passenger deck. It smells of cinnamon rolls, bleach, old coffee. Sylvie says she'll get everyone a cup and find them.

"You want a booth or a seat?" Anders asks, but Otto is already making his way toward the doors outside, and his son follows him, pushes open the swinging door to the wind just ahead of Otto.

The cold nearly knocks him over. Gust like a wallop. His son holds his arm.

They stand at the rail looking out on the water. From here it's black, opaque. The boat churns a froth that collides with the waves in a violent spray. Far off, the water isn't still but moving. It's gathering its breath, drawing up and releasing, pleating and purling, rising in one heave and then rushing away from itself.

Otto thinks, *I'm disassembling. I'm falling apart.* And then, *No.* A snag in that doubt—lucidity, reason. He is entirely intact. He's standing on a ferry deck beside his son. There's wind in his face. The sky is just going dark, as it does every evening. In another twelve hours, the day will break again, send its runners of light down from the heavens, reroot itself once more to the earth. *Light from light.* This is just time passing. This is just the usual chorus of night retelling the same story. Nothing's lost for good.

He hears Ilse's voice again, steady, sturdy, certain as always. *Everything passes, doesn't it?* she says. *You reconsider what's important. You find other things to do and love. You change. You keep going. That's life.*

Yes, he understands. That's it exactly. That's the whole of it. You keep going.

You keep going. You keep going. You keep going.

Open Water

Vera gets on the plane alone and takes the window seat without looking at the empty middle. She never canceled Jonas's ticket. This is the sort of task she feels least capable of managing—endless hours on the phone. She had a minute of guilt about the wasted expense, but now she's relieved not to have to sit beside a stranger. She wants the extra room. That's what she's been thinking since Jonas died: *I just need some room.*

"Pillow?" The flight attendant is a pert-faced woman Vera guesses to be about her daughter's age—28, maybe 30. She raises her eyebrows and extends a pillow sheathed in a disposable paper case. Vera takes it, trading her credit card for a plastic package that holds earbuds, a flimsy paper-covered neck pillow, and two foil packets containing antibacterial towelettes. As soon as the woman has trolleyed forward to the next row, Vera plugs into the sound of ocean waves and reclines her seat.

It's June, and the lozenge of the window is slick and gray with rain, but as the plane rolls forward and ascends, the clouds thicken, brighten, threaded with light from the inside. Soon the plane is entirely inside a white gulley in a landscape of glowing cumulous towers. And just as quickly as they materialized, the clouds vaporize into blue, blue atmosphere, and Vera is suspended, the plane swimming in the vast nothingness above the earth. She feels a warmth on both cheeks, like the palms of two hands, one on each cheekbone, pressing, and when she looks at her double in the reflection of the window glass, she sees that she's crying.

Two summers ago, just as the pandemic restrictions began to ease, Jonas took up open-water swimming. He needed a way to get out and feel alive again, he said. He'd let everything go, and he needed to reclaim his life.

"What's that mean?" she asked. "Reclaim your life? Have you forfeited it until now?" The language made it all seem like some big game he'd decided he was losing, and what was she supposed to feel about that, after everything?

"Oh, don't be wounded," he said. "We've all forfeited in the last year, haven't we? Except here we are on the other side, and now what?" They weren't sick, he told her—not yet anyway—and he was tired of living like an invalid, trapped in the house. He'd read about cold-water therapy and the correlation between immune health and swimming in water below sixty degrees Fahrenheit. It could only be beneficial. He found a polar bear club of other cold-water enthusiasts who gathered on the rocky shore of Puget Sound a few miles from where he and Vera lived. Each time he met with the group for an early morning dip, he came home flushed and fairly trilling. The adrenaline, Jonas told her, was unbelievable. Like the twenty minutes of buzz after downing a fantastic cocktail or the last half mile of a really good run. Like the best sex of your life. He felt years younger. He wanted to sing an aria or climb a mountain or take her to the bedroom, which is what he did. *Don't you want to feel this way all the time?* he asked afterward as they lay in the dark quiet of their bedroom, and she didn't know how to respond.

The truth was that she found the change in him alarming. He'd been even-keeled and stoic for as long as she'd known him, the metronomic beat to her occasional emotional plummets. It felt unsettling to see him so openly happy. Contentment was one thing. He'd always been good at contentment, a trait that she admired—maybe even envied. But contentment was not happiness. And the swing in him now, at this stage in their lives, felt disruptive to her. More than that, she didn't feel on the other side of anything herself. The isolation of the last year hadn't been new to her the way it had to him, and just because the shops were open again didn't mean she was suddenly connected. A person had to have had a claim to have lost it. It wasn't anything she could say to him. He'd have listened, but it wasn't anything she knew how to say.

Over drinks one evening, she'd confessed her worry to a woman friend, who responded by asking if Jonas had been to a doctor. Brain tumors could cause such personality alterations. So could affairs. He should get an MRI and an STI test. But Vera shook her head. No, she was sure; he wasn't sick, and he wasn't unfaithful. This was worse. It seemed to come from nowhere and to have no clear outcome. What doctor would understand her anyhow? *Help. My husband is happier than I've ever seen him.* It wasn't a valid complaint.

She decided her best course was to accept his change, or at least entertain the possibility of accepting it. On a Friday morning in October, she tugged on her swimming suit. There were maybe fifteen other swimmers already there when she and Jonas arrived on the beach—most of them over 60, just like Jonas. They had scaled back on work or retired completely since the pandemic began, and they needed something new—something social and yet safe—to remind them that they were still alive. Something to make them feel that life racing through their bodies the way lust or ambition or competition once had. All those desires were the hungers of the young, Jonas told her. They were gas with a flame—hot and beautiful for a flaming second, but quickly nothing. Now, though—out of the blue and later than he could have anticipated—there was this vigor. Real, pumping life, and he wanted more of it.

As they stood around on the shore, he grinned, high-fived the other swimmers. "See?" He leaned close to her. "Look at these people? Not a single sad sap among us." He was only in trunks, his chest bare. The swimming had winnowed the thickness he'd gathered in midlife, and now she could see muscle under his skin, like when she'd first met him, almost. And this was true of the others, too—people with old faces but bodies still lithe, color to their skin and tone to their arms. Jonas claimed one woman was 93, though Vera wondered aloud if that could really be true or if she was the group's designated advertisement for this fountain of youth nonsense. Snake oil in the form of an old lady.

"Give it a chance, V," he said, and he kissed her, the rasp of his unshaven jaw on her cheek.

Under the gray skies, the swimmers stripped. They stepped out of their boots and walked into the icy water.

Vera watched rather than plunging in alongside them. She kept her coat zipped to the chin and her hands stuffed in her pockets. It all seemed wildly naked and illicit, the pale moons of their faces bobbing above the waves of gray-green water. They whooped like drunk teenagers. There was a collective giddiness to it. Some dove down and came up spluttering, beaming, shining and wet headed. Others ambled at the shoreline for a while longer, their knees pinking as the chill rushed up their limbs. Eventually, though, they were all in the water and swimming toward their target. Twenty feet or so out, a string of buoys delineated the edge of the scuba park some local divers had built, and the polar bears' routine was to swim there and back once—enough exposure to jolt their bodies back to life, but not enough to shock them into real hypothermia.

"Come in!" Jonas called. He was on his back, treading water and waiting for her to join him, his arms moving beneath the water like two pale fish and his legs extended, his toes already purpling.

She wanted to, but she also didn't want to. It was cold enough standing dry on the beach. And what would come of this? The hard stone of her resistance shifted in her gut. She'd been sure she'd at least try it, but now that she was here at the water's edge, Jonas's desire for her to love exactly what he did annoyed her. Since when did they have to do everything together? That wasn't their marriage. She liked her mornings at home alone with a cup of coffee while he swam. The months of quarantine closed into the house together had been suffocating. Some days she'd wanted nothing more than for him to leave for work as he'd done all their life together so that she could be alone in the velvet silence of the empty house. She missed that more than anything else they'd lost. When he started swimming, she'd encouraged it in part because it bought her a couple hours alone every day. And, besides that, she had no intention of becoming his swimming pal. She could think of nothing worse, in fact, and yet if she showed any capacity for it, what were the chances she wouldn't be roped into joining every swim in the future?

"Vera!" he called again as she stood in her parka, watching their slow crawl toward the buoys. "Come on in! I'm freezing my balls off out here waiting for you!"

She let out a tight blossom of warm breath, dropped her coat and waded in.

The water was like a vise, closing its hand around the knots of her gut when the tide sloshed at her navel. By the time she was in up to her collarbone, she could hardly catch a full breath. Everything in her seized. She was made of metal, her bones clanging inside her skin as she stroked her way out to the buoys and back, crawling fast, quickly ahead of him. *There*, she thought. *Done.* She'd tried it, and now the whole thing could be behind her.

She recognized the thought as small and miserly, not at all the openness she wished she were capable of conjuring, but it was what she could give.

At the shore again, she tugged on her coat, fumbling in the heap of Jonas's jeans for his car keys with numb fingers, and marched to the parking lot, furious—with him and with herself. When he came after her, she was in the passenger seat with the motor running and the heat blowing at its highest setting, her body an angry cramp.

"We're very different people," she said.

She saw the soft slackening of his happiness, which, in spite of herself, pleased her.

"Yes," he said. "I guess so. But you could try, V." There was disappointment in his voice, but—worse than that—resignation. A ripple of regret trickled through her.

They didn't get out again to join the others on the beach with their thermoses of coffee. Jonas honked once in good-bye, and they pulled out of the beach lot.

When the plane judders into its descent in Çanakkale, Vera jars and realizes she's been sleeping. She's had the dream that's been recurring in one form or another since Jonas died—a dream in which she is at once underwater and also flying. It makes no sense, but she finds it neither terrifying nor pleasurable, just odd. Sitting up now, she peels back her mask to wipe away a slick of drool from her chin. She's disoriented, but the rushing sound in her ears is just the endless loop of sea sounds she's had playing in her earbuds since takeoff, the constriction at her hips is the seat belt. Her head slurs with that slop-and-drag feeling of deep sleep's tide receding, the last grip of that hand on her face makes her cheek burn hot. *Who is it?* She thinks it, but she already knows. Of course she knows. She rubs her temples and tucks her hair behind her ears. She doesn't want Ari seeing her a mess when she disembarks. She won't cry in front of her daughter.

Ari is flying in separately, from Berlin, where she's living with a man Vera's never met—a fellow designer Ari worked with online through the lockdown. When the borders opened again, he invited her to Germany, and she went.

"You're moving in with him, sight unseen?" Vera had said over the phone.

"I've seen him, Mother. Jesus. You act like there's another way people meet now. And, seriously, what do I have to lose at this point?"

What a ridiculous question! Vera thought, and, as if the gate between her mind and her mouth had sprung open, she simply said it: "What a ridiculous question."

She heard Ari's sigh.

"Why do you have to judge everything?" Ari said. "Don't you want me to be happy?"

"Of course I want you to be happy. But where can an internet romance possibly go in the long run?"

"Who even knows if there's a long run right now?" There was an edge of frustration in her voice, as if Vera couldn't understand what it was to be young in this strange period of time when mortality hung between every moment like an exhaled breath.

"Don't say that. Don't you want a long run?"

"Like you and Dad, you mean?"

"What does that mean?"

How was it that a daughter always knew just where to dig to make the deepest puncture?

"I don't think like you," Ari said.

"Are you thinking at all? This is a stranger you're ready to just move in with."

"Mom. That's enough."

"You're being impulsive," Vera said.

Ari had hung up, and Vera had stood, like a woman in a cartoon, the dead phone still pressed to her ear.

That was early autumn of last year, and they hadn't spoken again until winter, when Vera had called Ari in Berlin to tell her that her father was dead. Now it was spring, and they still hadn't seen one another; Jonas hadn't wanted a funeral, and so Vera hadn't held one, and so Ari had not come home. It felt like a breach, though. Like another cut. She should have come home, Vera thought, not for her father but for Vera. If the German had died, even though she'd never met him, Vera would have gone to be at Ari's side. Ari, the only child. Ari, the beloved girl. The distance between them, which had always been there but had really begun widening when Ari was a teenager, felt to Vera like a rust, slowly corrosive. It left her with a hollow space, a pain where she'd once carried Ari, low in her center.

Jonas hadn't understood. His relationship with Ari was different, close and easy and certain. When Ari had gone to Germany, Jonas had chided Vera for her stubbornness. "Just call her," he'd said again and again. He himself was calling. Vera had heard him on the phone late at night, which was early in the morning for Ari across the world. "Call your mother, please," she heard him say once, but Ari hadn't called, and because she didn't, Vera couldn't. And then Jonas was gone, and there was no bridge between mother and daughter anymore.

Now, in the airport, Vera meets her daughter at the baggage claim. Ari carries her body the same way Jonas did—with a loose, easy habitation of her own skin. She's in a cropped black T-shirt and a slim white skirt. Her hair, which was blond just like her father's was, she's dyed a pale pink, and she's woven it in a braid that rings her head. When she's close enough, Vera sees that the deep U of her shirt's neckline reveals a scoop of freckled skin—the last vestigial glitter of her childhood rising to the surface of this woman she's become—and on top of the freckles, a tattoo that begins at the center of her chest and opens out, two delicate wings in blue ink following the lines of her collar bones.

"This is new," Vera says, pointing.

"Nice to see you too." Ari frowns, shrugs. "It's for Daddy. You know. Waves."

Vera sees now that it is waves, not wings. The fragile lines she mistook for feathers are the tiny arcs of wind across water. She wonders at this choice and what Jonas would think of it. Their daughter has marked herself permanently in homage to him.

"It's good to see you, Munch," is all she says, withholding the rest. *Munch*—a term of endearment left over from Ari's babyhood. Munch like munchkin, which was Jonas's pet name for her originally, and in time just her home name. The familiarity softens them both. Vera reaches for a hug, and Ari leans forward. Her bare cheek touches Vera's paper mask in a mock kiss. For a moment they clasp each other.

It's Ari who pulls away first. "Your flight was late," she says. "I've been here for literally hours." Her exhale smells of mint gum and what Vera thinks is an undercurrent of weed. "Can we just go already?" She gestures at the pile of bags bumping together on the carousel.

Vera scans and doesn't see her suitcase.

The carousel circles twice more, and finally Ari leaves to get the car while Vera queues with a line of others at a customer service window to file a lost bag form. There's a man at the front, pounding his fist on the counter and shouting in French. A young dark-haired woman with a flat expression waits until he pauses before translating what he's said to her colleague at the computer. This takes several minutes, but finally they hand the angry passenger a piece of paper and he leaves, cursing under his breath. When it's Vera's turn, the woman merely lifts her eyebrows archly and sighs. She's given the same piece of paper the man ahead of her received—a receipt confirming her flight number and lost luggage. A promise to call her when her bag turns up, though she knows it never will. It's vanished somewhere between Seattle and Turkey, in the gut of the wrong plane or in a backroom of the wrong airport or in the trunk of some airline employee's car. She closes her eyes. The bag is gone, not hers anymore. She has to let it go. The lacing of anxiety in her chest loosens.

She walks through the baggage claim's sliding doors and out into the dry spring warmth. Without her checked bag, all she has is her carry-on duffel, in which she has packed—ridiculously—just a book and a swimming suit that she meant to wear into the Çanakkale Strait, the Strait of Gallipoli, the Dardanelles, Hellespont—waterway of too many names. This trip was Jonas's plan—a flight across the world to swim the famous crossing. He wanted her there on the far shore, cheering him on, the Hero to his Leander. And now she's here with no change of clothes and no real sense of where she is or where she's going, no desire to get into the water he wanted for himself. There's a hilarity in it that makes her feel woozy, or giddy—like her head might lift off her neck and float off into the ether. Is this what Jonas felt coming up from the cold water for a gulp of air? She squints. The light here is brighter than even the brightest day at home, no veil of clouds. It flashes off the car windows of the parking lot and spangles in chains from the massive windows of the airport terminals. She drops her sunglasses to her face again and lets out a long, counted breath.

She's doing just this—staring through the blued filter of her glasses and breathing in even rhythm—when Ari pulls to the curb. "God, Mom," she says through her open window. "What's going on with you? You're just standing here. I thought you were coming out to the lot."

"How would I know where to look for anyone here?" She folds herself into the passenger seat of the European minicar rental and Ari looks at her once, a frown Vera sees from the periphery of her vision and ignores.

Eventually, Jonas wanted more than the polar dips, and that's when he began open-water swimming. At first he just swam beyond the buoy line. Next, the length of the full shore. He drove to Lake Washington and spent a day swimming there, swam a section of the Snohomish River, a bay up north at Deception Pass. He swam the Little Bear Creek that spring when its waters were high and tumbling, though he could still stand and touch its grassy bottom any time he chose, he said. He read books about other open-water swimmers. A Brit who swam the Strait of Gibraltar in the 1920s, a German who crossed the Baltic Sea, several people who circumnavigated Manhattan Island at various points in history, and—his favorite—Lord Byron, who swam the Hellespont in 1810. He dreamed about this last one, woke up with water running off his face and a chill in his chest that only being against her in bed could cure, he said. He grinned in the low light of dawn, rolling Vera onto her back and kissing her chest, her neck, her mouth, the spot behind each ear.

Sometimes, though, it was Vera who startled awake beside him to the sound of him gasping, his mouth gulping at the dry air in the dark middle of the night. *Jonas*, she'd say, a whisper at first. *Jonas!* She shook him until he sputtered, sat up gulping breath. What was wrong with him? She put her hands on his face, his chest, felt his heart beating regular and even through his rib cage. He'd terrified her. But, no. He was fine, he reassured her. He was dreaming—just dreaming.

Within moments he was back asleep, peaceful beside her as she lay with her eyes on the ceiling, her heart still pounding in her chest. Where had he been in his dream? Somewhere far from home, laps away from any safe shore.

"Come swim with me," he always invited her in the morning as he rolled up his towel and prepared for his daily swim, but she never did. She resented the water the way another woman would have resented a mistress.

At the rental apartment, there are only two bedrooms, and Vera claims the one facing the street and closes its door before there can be any discussion about it. She's jetlagged and worn. The episode in the parking lot—whatever it was—has left her jellied and woozy, and she feels a wave of sleep approaching, the lip of fatigue bubbling at the base of her neck like a low-grade headache. She fishes a Tylenol PM from her bag, downs it dry, and slips off her shoes.

She immediately falls into dreaming, and when she wakes, the same dream again hangs like vapor in her head, gauzy and impossible to catch or make sense of. A feeling like déjà vu. Whatever it is she's seeing behind her eyes while she sleeps, she can almost remember when she wakes up, and then it's gone. It's the feeling of seeing from the corner of her eye a reflection in a storefront window and recognizing the woman there before realizing it's her own face she sees. There's a bifurcation. A sense of another reality circling her, splitting from her own and winding another way. *Whose life is she living?* It makes her question. The therapist she saw for a couple of months after Jonas died told her she was simply processing her trauma, that her brain was trying to reassure itself in this new world—that is, the world-without-Jonas.

Maybe.

Vera reminds herself: *You are in the apartment with Ari.* She sits up slowly and lets the initial vertigo spin itself to nothing, puts her feet onto the tiles of the bedroom floor. A shock of cold runs like a current up both shins. *What time is it?* She looks for a clock but can't find one, nor her watch, which she's somehow misplaced, though she can't imagine how.

At the window she opens the shutters. It's night outside. Slices of moonlight cut between the close shoulders of the apartment buildings that line the street. She hears music, but from where? A low thumping bass and the distant and indistinct chatter of a crowd. She didn't pay attention to the neighborhood on her way in, and now it's hard to see. There's the luxurious warm-climate scent of jasmine blooms and mock orange on the air. She thinks it must be eight or so, but soon remembers that it is June, just past solstice, and darkness doesn't even fall until later than that. Her blouse is on the floor and her trousers strewn across the desk chair. She can't remember sliding out of them, but she must have. She stuffs her feet into her shoes and soft-foots it through the apartment before realizing it is empty—Ari has gone out and left her to sleep. There's no food in the cabinets, no wine on the counter, so she finds her key and her jacket and leaves, texting Ari on her way: *Where can I find you?*

Outside, the air is cooler than she expects. She walks to the end of the block and turns, deciding left rather than right purely on instinct, following the music. She passes a man leaning in his doorway, smoking a cigarette, the tip a hot pink-orange spot like a bit of melting candy. He appraises her with slow eyes, and she hurries her footsteps away from him. In front of another door, a couple are wound around each other. Vera is intensely aware of herself as a woman alone in the dark, but she doesn't turn back, and soon enough she's on a street of shops, some of them barred closed for the night, but many still open, their lights blazing and their sidewalk tables full of people eating and drinking. The music is from a town square another block away. Here, all the shops are open and a crowd is gathered, some dancing, some clustered in groups, talking and smoking. Tiny globe lights on a string dangle overhead, and a modular stage has been set up in the center. A band plays rock music in a language she doesn't know. The singer is a man with long hair and leather pants. He tosses his head back in a final note and the square erupts in applause. She looks for a tall, slim woman with pink hair, but Ari is nowhere.

At a bar on the corner, Vera steps inside. The place is drowned in blue light and heavy with smoke. It smells of cologne and sweat and alcohol, and under that an iron-and-sweetness odor that could be rose hips on the bushes outside or sex here on the dance floor inside. She pushes herself forward to the bar, orders a cocktail in English. "Just whatever you'd drink," she tells the bartender, and he hands her a tall, slim glass of cloudy liquid. It tastes like anise and spreads ribbons of warmth through her chest and around her back. She's thirsty. When was the last time she drank anything? On the plane she had a soda water. That was hours ago. She orders a second and a plate of flat bread, stands at the bar devouring, gulping.

"How far from here to the water?" she asks the bartender when he passes her again, but he shakes his head, taps his ear.

"He doesn't speak English," says a man on the stool next to hers. He smiles. He's younger—maybe 50—and attractive. "It's not far though. An easy walk." She looks at him—maybe too closely, because his smile broadens, and he pats the seat of the stool beside his own. "Sit," he says. "It's bad for your stomach to eat standing up."

"I'm not staying," she says.

"Why do Americans always want to rush? Do you eat standing up at home?" His voice is warm, edged in kindness. French accent. He's ribbing her. Flirting.

"We do," she says. "We have troughs, actually, instead of dining tables."

He laughs, and she flushes.

"You're funny," he says. "More people need to laugh at themselves."

She sits.

"You're going to the water after this?"

"It was just curiosity," she says. "I'm here with my daughter."

"No, no. You should see it. There's a moon tonight. You have a camera?"

She has her phone, she tells him, and he wrinkles his nose in distaste.

"No matter," he says. "You have eyes."

He's up on his feet and extending his hand. His name is Didier, he tells her. "Let's go."

"My daughter—"

"You have a phone, you said. You text her where we'll be."

She hesitates, but—surprising herself—she follows him out of the bar.

The winter Ari was 11, Jonas spent a quarter in Rome on his own. He'd been invited to teach a course through the university's international program, and at first they'd thought the three of them would all go, but Ari fell ill with mono the week before the trip, and it was suddenly impossible. He left, and Vera used her own banked sick days to stay home from work, solo parenting Ari through the early days of the virus, the two of them quarantined together, just like when Ari was a newborn and Vera was on maternity leave. The hours were long and still. Ari slept. She ran a high fever for nine full days, and for the rest of the month was simply fatigued, her neck a little tender and swollen where her lymph nodes worked to heal her, her breath rapid when she got up from the couch. It terrified Vera to see her so sick, but the doctor assured her it would pass and Ari would recover. They just had to wait.

In the middle of the third week, on a trip to the pharmacy, Vera paused to look at the adjacent pet store's window, which was full of bird cages. Inside the cages powder-blue and bright-yellow and spring-green parakeets tittered and chucked their heads. They swung on their suspended bars and picked at sticks rolled in seeds. Vera thought of her Swedish grandmother, who'd kept a parakeet in a cage in her kitchen in Stockholm until her death, claiming the bird made winter bearable. On visits there as a child, Vera was fascinated by the bird, but also afraid of it. Now and then her grandmother let it out of the cage, and it flew around the house, alighting on the top of the bookcase or the crown of the domed lamp over the dining table. It pooped on a newspaper her grandmother replaced in the bottom of its cage every morning and tossed its seeds onto the floor below the cage, making a mess. But it was also beautiful, its body and wings baby blue and its head a pretty yellow.

She went into the pet store with such a bird in mind for Ari—a companion for the recovery she had ahead of her, and the Seattle winter, which could be as steely and dark as Stockholm's. But once in the store, she remembered the smell of the bird, the dust it made, and she came out instead with an empty aquarium bowl and a bag of water holding a large snail.

At home Ari delighted in the snail. Artemis, she named her. Vera set up the aquarium on Ari's bedside table where she could watch the snail as she lay recuperating, and the snail was beautiful, her shell brown and white and golden and her soft tentacles wavering in the water. Artemis liked to climb the glass of the aquarium wall, which sheened with a brown fuzz between cleanings, the lapping hole of her mouth moving in repetitive circles as she devoured the skim of her own mess. *Housekeeping*, Vera called it, and Ari laughed. Artemis had a trick, too, which they both found mesmerizing. She climbed the plants to perch at the top, the flat foot of her body pressed against the glass and pulsing, the dome of her pearlescent shell clear of the waterline. Like she wanted the air up there. Like her whole body had become a tongue she could use to lap in the light. She often clung to the glass for long minutes that way, the frilled brown lip of her body undulating against the tank, until, for no obvious reason but pleasure, she released her hold and parachuted back down to the tank's floor, her flesh a satin wing that caught the drag of the water. Rather glorious, Vera had thought the first time she saw it, and every time after, too.

It was also during this long winter, while Jonas was still away but after Ari was well enough to return to school, that Vera began seeing someone else. The man was someone she worked with. He was kind and not unattractive, and Vera was lonely. The loneliness wasn't the reason she invited this man into her life, though. Loneliness was bearable, expected even. No, it was something else that made her choose him, some longing she couldn't name. A vacancy beneath her feet at every moment, and the feeling that the next step might drop her into a chasm she couldn't see. She felt terrified, but not of anything in particular. *Why am I so anxious?* she asked herself, and she couldn't name a cause for the feeling, couldn't find a way through the perpetual sensation that she was about to lose her grip on everything. The man presented himself as a bridge. When she was with him, she felt a melancholic freedom from herself, the complicated relief of getting outside her own skin. She decided not to try to understand the choice, and there was relief in that, too. The man came home with her at lunch a few times, and it was fine until one afternoon they fell asleep in bed and woke up to the sound of Ari letting herself in the front door downstairs, home from school.

"Oh shit," he whispered.

"No," she said. She thought quickly, and a sense of clarity came to her. It was as if she were watching the pieces of a puzzle sliding neatly together beneath her fingertips. "My daughter is a child. She won't understand. Just don't make a thing of it." A calm washed through her, and she got up and pulled on clothes. "Wait ten minutes and leave through the front door. Act like nothing's wrong." She went downstairs to make Ari an after-school snack.

When he appeared at the end of the hallway between the kitchen and the front door, he paused, his face pale with guilt and the horror of having been caught.

"See you!" Vera waved, though, her voice high and lilting, as it would have been if she'd bumped into an old friend at the grocery store or a client at the gym.

"Oh," he said. A wounded expression crossed his face, and she recognized it as the guilt he would now carry, having seen her daughter. That would have to be his business to work out, though; she'd never see him again, she already knew, except at work, where they'd be cordial and no more. "Sure thing," he said. He left, his jacket over his arm, and she saw Ari's eyes follow him as he crossed the lawn to his car parked on the side street rather than taking the front walk.

"Who was that?" Ari asked.

"Just someone from work. But the workday is over now, isn't it? I'm sure he's going home to have dinner, which is what I should get started here too." She smiled and offered no more explanation, and because she didn't, Ari didn't ask any more questions. *Children are like that*, Vera thought. The world is full of confusions and perplexities for them, and so they absorb whatever they encounter without the ability to translate it. She'd banked on it.

The next morning, though, passing through the house on her way out the door, she saw that Ari had brought the snail downstairs and left the aquarium bowl on the dining room's sideboard, and she knew she'd miscalculated.

Soon it was March, the end of the quarter. Jonas came home, and Ari's complete devotion to him might have been the natural result of his absence, or it might have been Vera's punishment. Who could say? Vera settled long ago to never knowing. What difference would knowing make? *I've been who I could be*, she often said to herself when she began to worry about her relationship with her daughter. She decided neither to hate herself nor to forgive her failures as a mother, a wife, a woman. She'd done what she'd done, and that was all. Mistakes and victories all end in the same future anyhow, which is moving on.

At the beach the Çanakkale night sky is thick with ambient city light, and the suspension bridge that spans the channel to connect this side with the European side is lit bright and doubled in the water. "I thought there would be more visible stars here," Vera says. "More than at home, I mean."

"People imagine this place as if no time has passed here," Didier says. "They think they're going back to Troy." He laughs. "They arrive wanting to see Odysseus and Helen. Time travel, they think. As if this place has been preserved, just for them." Another laugh, snobbish edge to it.

She says, "I don't think that. I didn't come here for the past."

This gets a raise of his eyebrows. "No?" he asks. "You don't care for the history?"

She smirks, flirting in return. "Oh, I see how it is with you. Damned if I do, and damned if I don't."

He crows with laughter. "A joke! You're joking. See, I told you you're funny. I like that. A woman with humor." He inches closer to her, lays a hand on her knee that she doesn't protest. "But, truly," he says, "let me ask you in seriousness: Why are you here if not that?"

She doesn't want to explain herself. "My daughter lives in Germany. This is a middle ground for us, you could say. An in-between place."

The answers softens the margin between them again. She feels his thumb drawing circles on the inside of her thigh.

He, too, landed here because it was between two places. His ex-wife was Israeli; he is from Strasbourg. They moved here, split up, and he stayed. This has become home. "Not by birth, just by claim," he says. His hand is warm. It sends a rill of goosebumps up her thigh.

"By claim," she repeats. "So you're more like Paris than like Odysseus." It's a poke at him, seduction if he reads it right, as Jonas would have, but he doesn't.

"Claim, yes," he says. "Home by claim. This means—"

"No, I understand you." She cuts him off, disappointed. Like a gust of breeze, her grief.

"We're not translating each other, perhaps," he says. He's frowning.

"It's just—Paris, I mean, he—" She pauses. She's tired. The words are blocks of wood, filling her mouth. Does she care enough to try again? She thinks of that cold water turning her bones to metal rods when she swam out ahead of Jonas. She says, "Men are always claiming things, aren't they?" It isn't what she means, though. Comes out sounding feminist, political, offended. And, yes—*Yes to all of that*, she thinks; but it's not what she means right now. She puts her head in her hands.

He withdraws his hand from her knee and the space where it's been feels colder than if he'd never touched her at all.

He says, "It's not easy to be caught in between."

"Right," she says.

What will happen next, she already knows. She'll tell him it's late, and she should go, and when she gets up to leave, he'll say something kind or something callous—it won't matter, because either way she'll come off prickly, joyless. A woman who can't let the moment swell and glitter the way he's hoped it would. A woman who has disappointed his expectations and her own, too. And she won't have the words for what does actually glitter inside her—the crackling zip of her own anger, like a sparkler lit and fizzing in the soft center of her sternum, just beneath her bones. *Is it anger? Yes*, she thinks. *Anger, and also fear.* One and the same sometimes. Most times. Small and hissing. Bright and burning, but only dangerous when held too close.

The water laps and laps at the beach with a quiet smacking sound, a little sensual, a little like the suck of a baby at the nipple. She remembers nursing Ari and marveling at the greedy desire with which such a tiny baby could eat. It could look like fury, that hunger. The child, Vera sometimes thought, wanted nothing less than to devour her. It was a shameful thought. Ari had come late to her and Jonas. Vera was nearly 40 when she finally got pregnant after ten years of trying. Forty was late for motherhood in her generation. Not so much now, she knows. She felt old, though. She had trouble trusting that her body would know what to do, and once Ari arrived, she felt the birth as a dividing line in her life—a line she'd long imagined crossing, but once she had crossed it and was a mother, she couldn't go back. It felt like she'd lost something. Each time she nursed the baby, she felt a sudden shuddering rush, an electric pain in both her breasts, and, finally, arousal. It was as if those two sides of herself—the woman she'd been before and the woman she became after Ari's birth were colliding, and it was disorienting, shameful. The collision, irrationally, made her angry—a shivering, tremoring, glittering anger that vibrated through her so that she feared she'd shake the child. Could she trust herself? And who was she angry with, anyway? Her baby? Herself? What kind of mother feels angry nursing her child? She never understood, and so she learned to manage it by dissociating for the few minutes it took her to feed her daughter. She'd give Ari her breast and step outside of her own skin to wait nearby until the meal was over. She never said this to anyone, even to Jonas. How could she have? How could she when she was being so selfish to feel uncomfortable about feeding her own child? It was the beginning of their divergence, she thinks now—her not telling him, him not knowing her. A channel opened between them—a mirror of the one that she felt within her own self—and it never closed after that. Never, though only she was aware of this fissure. She thinks now about what Didier has said—that people come here wanting ancient history. Somewhere in this town is a massive Trojan horse replica. She read about it in the travel guides Jonas bought for the trip. This history is a fiction though, and maybe every history is, the true story nested and waiting inside the shell that memory makes to encase it.

To Didier, she turns. "Did I tell you already that I was supposed to watch someone swim across this waterway?"

"Ridiculous." Despite the uncertainty in his voice, he returns his hand to her knee, and this time she reaches up and pulls him toward her, kisses him. She can feel the warmth of his breath in her mouth, in her throat, in her lungs. He slides his hand along the length of her body, up her thigh and under her blouse, and holds her there at her ribcage, a half embrace that becomes a grip, and at first she thinks she wants it, and then she knows she doesn't.

"I'm sorry," she says, pulling back. "I misunderstood."

Across the water the lights track slicks of color against the darkness. She starts to stand, but he stops her, puts his hand on the small of her back now.

"Did you want something else?" he asks. "Maybe it was I who misunderstood."

She feels foolish. "I'm not sure." This is the truth. She thought she'd know herself better by now, but she still can't explain what she wants or doesn't or why. "I'm a widow," she says. "I don't know if I told you. I miss my husband all the time." She recognizes it as the truth.

"Ah," he says. He stands and puts his hands into his pockets.

"I'm sorry," she says again, though she wants to stop apologizing.

"No," he tells her. "I'll go."

She watches him leave.

Down the beach a group of young people have a portable speaker. Vera's been ignoring them, but now she's alone and her attention is frayed. Their music is loud. To her ears it is beautiful but also chaotic. She picks out the stringed sound of a baglama and the fluttering of flutes. The revelers wave glowing plastic sticks from both hands in time to the music's rhythm. Some have lit their cell phone flashlights, whose beams arc and vanish, catching as they pass her a woman at the center of the festivities. The woman is Hula-Hooping. Three wide, glow-in-the-dark hoops circle and circle her body, their twirling lit in streaks of color, mesmerizing in the darkness. The woman herself might be made of shadow, though when the light of the phones skims her skin, she appears golden. There's a chain around her bare abdomen, and it catches the light and glitters. She might be a goddess, or a mirage. She might be Helen herself.

When Vera read *The Odyssey* and *The Iliad* as an undergraduate, she found Helen selfish. What woman would leave her husband and daughter and run off with a young man? At the time the allure of such a tryst—the risk of it—was unfathomable to her. She was 20 and had just met Jonas, who was two years older. She wanted him. She could not imagine ever wanting anything else so completely. Just holding his hand to cross the campus lawn left her in a state for the rest of the day. She fantasized about licking his Adam's apple, about the bristle of his cheek against her thigh. She nearly failed a class that term. The idea of wanting any life other than one spent at his side and in his bed was impossible to her before she had that life.

A long moment passes before Vera's eyes perceive that the woman at the center of the circle is Ari. Ari's hair is down now, long waves that reach the small of her back. She's wearing a bikini top and a sarong. When the song ends, everyone claps, and Ari stills. The hoops fall to her feet. She's laughing, smiling. A man who has been sitting on the sand stands and pulls her toward him, and Ari kisses him, lifting one of her legs and hooking him close. The sarong falls away, and Vera turns her head. It's suddenly too personal a scene, though the other partiers are all there. Vera feels as if she's walked in on her daughter, alone with a lover. She gets up and leaves the beach, and it isn't until morning that she sees Ari again, there at the little table in the apartment when Vera wakes up.

"Out late?" Vera asks. Ari is still in the sarong, though now she has a sweatshirt over it, the hood pulled up over her head. Her eyes are tired, makeup rounding shadows on her cheekbones.

"I couldn't sleep."

"Right."

"What about you? When did you finally get up? I came back for a bit in the evening, and you were gone."

"I got hungry. I found a place."

Vera pours coffee and sits. The late-morning light is soft here, almost orange. Again, she feels the weight of a hand at her chest, at her cheek, and she knows. She says, "I'm lying. I was up. I saw you on the beach. It just seemed like not my business." The pressure eases.

"It was a celebration of life," Ari says.

"A what?"

"There was no funeral. You didn't bring ashes. I mentioned it to some people I met at a bar, and they suggested the beach. It was nice to have people care about him."

Vera doesn't know what to say to this. "With strangers?" she asks.

"Are you upset?" The question is goading. Ari meets Vera's eyes—a challenge. She holds her coffee the way her father always did, Vera recognizes, both hands around the cup as if she's won it. Without makeup she looks like him too. She didn't always look like him, though as she aged and the baby softness fell away, there he was—his jawline, his brow, his eyes in their daughter's face. Vera has understood this, too, as part of Ari's attachment to her father. What must it be to see your own eyes in another face? What must it be to watch yourself age and pass away while you're still in your own youth? She has no idea about that kind of closeness. She has only ever been herself.

"Are you leaving him, your German?" she asks Ari.

"Why would you think that?"

"The kiss. That wasn't him, was it? I assumed it wasn't him."

Ari smiles. "That's such an old-fashioned way to think about things. You think because you saw me kiss someone else on the beach, I have to leave Markus?" She shakes her head.

Vera lays her hands on the table. "Does it have to be this way with us, still? I didn't mean to be laughable. I can leave it, if you'd rather not say."

"God, Mother. Don't do that. You always get hurt by anything you don't understand."

You think I don't understand that? she wants to say. "I do?" she says instead though.

After a moment Ari gets up, runs water in her mug. From the sink she says, "It doesn't matter. I've already left him." She hasn't been in Berlin for weeks, she says. She's been traveling. Paris, Copenhagen, Athens. She can work from anywhere. "I sort of fell apart," she says.

"What? You what?"

"After Daddy. I just—" She raises her hands, and they hover close to her face, as if she's about to cover a sob. Vera knows this gesture, or the feeling it represents. It's the nearness of the grief, and grief's restlessness. The way the loss veils everything. Jonas is bigger in death than he was in life, and so is her love for him, and so are the ways she hurt him. She's under the shadow of it all the time now that he's gone. She can't explain this to her daughter. Even if she wanted to, she can't explain it.

Vera says, "I wish you had come home. When your father died, I wish you had felt that you could come home."

"I did, actually." Ari turns. Her hands are still wet from the faucet, and she wipes them on her sweatshirt. "Last month. I was home for a week. I got a room, and I went to the beach, and I tried to be present again in the places he took me—the places that meant something to us both."

"But you didn't tell me." Vera is breathless.

"I can't apologize for it, Mom, if that's what you want."

The admission is a blade in her side, the cut cold and neat. Deserved. She swallows against the ache of it. "No," she finally says. "You shouldn't have to apologize."

Vera sees this: Ari at the beach where Jonas swam, the March sky rubbed white by the last of winter's chill, and the forsythia at the edge of beach lot a flaming gold line. She might have passed her there and not even known, like strangers. Again, she feels that pressure and pull at her cheek, her chest, and thinks that this is how her daughter will finally devour her: the longing of the infant for the mother inverted now.

Vera pushes up from her chair and leaves her mug on the table. "I'm going to wash my face," she says. "And maybe lie down. I'm so tired." She leaves the room and is behind her own door before she's crying.

Does it matter how he died? Vera hasn't thought it necessary to tell her daughter the details. To Ari she said it was a heart attack, quick, and that is true. But it happened in the water. A morning swim in the cold, half a mile up the shore from the beach where he'd waded in. He had an orange float tied to his waist, as they all did. Another swimmer saw him flagging. She yelled, and they all stopped and lapped their way toward him. It took four of them to pull him to the beach, which was rocky along that stretch of the shoreline. Someone called the paramedics from a smart watch. Someone else did CPR. Vera herself wasn't called until it was all over, and by the time she saw him, he was on a gurney, a sheet over his body. His face was already a mask of itself. As she walked out of the hospital, she felt him behind her, whatever it was of him that refused to be done. She got into the car, and he got in beside her. She drove home with his hand on her knee. She went inside and got into bed, and he got in beside her, curled his body around her, but still, she couldn't get warm. A whole day and a night and another day passed before she got hungry enough to get out of bed, and by then she felt certain that he was waiting for her to tell him to go, and so she did, yelling into the sudden vastness of the house: "Go!" She didn't tell her daughter any of this when she called, only that he was gone, that there was nothing anybody could do. It wasn't a kindness. It was a way of keeping what she had of him. It was a way of protecting the little that was hers, small as that made her.

At midday Ari calls from the other side of the closed door that she's going to the beach, and Vera hesitates but decides she should try, and so they go together, swimming suits under their clothes, towels from the apartment's bathroom over their arms, both of them silent as they pass through the quiet afternoon streets.

Vera isn't sure she'll swim until they're at the beach. "You have to go in," Ari says. "You've come all this way. And it's what he wanted." She herself drops the sarong, which she's worn as a dress this time, and crosses the beach in long strides, diving in and coming up in a crawl stroke several yards out, her wet head shining and a grin on her face. Vera watches her. It's performance and ritual, both, as Ari laps through the water, beaming, ducking her head beneath the surface again and again, as if she can wash meaning into the cavity of her loss. As if performing finality will make her feel it. She's too young to know otherwise, and the other anchors of meaning have no gravity for her, Vera supposes. Everything is ephemeral, uncertain for her generation. It's trite but true. Ari's longing isn't about grasping the present; it's about her fear that there's nothing other than the present. The past and the future both are porous and fragile and too tender to survive. Vera watches her daughter swim. Confident strokes. When she turns her face to breathe, the water runs from her head in fiery, sparkling streams. Glorious, the light on her face, Vera thinks. Glorious, this girl she and Jonas made—one victory, at least, despite their many failures.

"Are you getting in?" Ari yells to the shore where Vera stands.

Vera takes off her shoes and walks into the water. It's clear and strung with light and warmer than she expects it to be. She looks at her feet and steps forward. Steps forward. The water laps at her shins.

"Mom!" Ari calls, and there's affection in the way she says it, Vera thinks. She hears affection in it. She waves at her daughter. She wants the water to mean more too. She wants it to open her up again. It comes to her that she did love him. She loved him more than she knew she could love. Is this enough?

Submerging her back, her shoulders, she spreads her arms and her legs like she could take the water into herself, like she's hungry for the current.

Acknowledgments

Many of the stories included here were previously published in journals. "Revision" was published in *Michigan Quarterly Review* (summer 2019); "At the Last" was published in *On the Seawall* (February 2020); "Eclipse" was published in *McSweeney's Quarterly Concern*, issue 61 (fall 2020); "Outer Stars" appeared in *Prairie Schooner's* summer 2022 issue; "Clean Breaks" appeared in *The Sun* in the summer of 2024; and "Wind Phone" was published in *Conjunctions* online in October of 2024. My gratitude to these journals and their editorial staffs—including, in particular, Polly Rosenwaike, Khaled Mattawa, Hannah Webster, Ron Slate, Nancy Holochwost, Andrew Snee, Seth Mirsky, Claire Boyle, Siwar Masannat, and Bradford Morrow—is immense. Thank you all so much for the ways your expert readings and suggestions improved my work, and thank you for giving these stories their first homes. Additionally, a million thanks to Jody Kahn and Gail Hochman for shepherding many of these narratives toward their readers and for your invaluable support of the collection. You're the best, and I'm so lucky to have you both in my corner.

Thank you to Polly Buckingham, the University of North Texas, and the Katherine Ann Porter Prize judges and editorial team. What a dream and honor it is to have my collection bear the name of the fierce and wonderful Porter.

This collection was also supported by my workshop with Laura van den Berg at the 2021 Tin House Summer Workshop and a residency through the Willa Cather Foundation in the fall of 2023. Thank you to these organizations, as well as to Jane Hodges and the Mineral School, for the time and focus necessary to write. Gratitude to Pam Houston, always and forever.

Boundless thanks to Kristen Millares Young, Jean Ferruzola, and Patricia Henley for their patience, collaboration, support, and encouragement as my first readers. I am so grateful to be in the embrace of your brilliance and friendship.

Thank you, as ever, to my students and colleagues at The Bush School and Hugo House in Seattle, who keep my daily life lively, who teach me so much about existing as a human and a reader and a writer and a teacher, and who make me feel welcome and valued in our learning communities. To be among you is a true gift.

Thank you to my extended families—the whole Lunstrum bunch (no one is luckier in in-laws than I am), the original Wilkies and Sundbergs and the ones they've added to our circle, and the friends who feel like family. You know who you are and how much I love you. Thank you to Tamara, always my dearest, for so many years of friendship and conversation. Norma, a galaxy of gratitude for parenting alongside me. Hannah, thank for the hours of coffee and kindness and talking it all through. I'm so glad to know you.

Finally, gratitude forever and ever to my truest true loves, my beloveds, my sky and my sea, the people who have taught me so much about what it is to live: Paul, Dorinda, Britt, Nathan, Finn, and Virginia. Thank you, thank you, thank you. I cannot be without you.